NASCAR®

SECRETS and LEGENDS

OVERHEATED
by Barbara Dunlop

From the opening green flag at Daytona to the final checkered flag at Homestead, the competition will be fierce for the NASCAR Sprint Cup Series championship.

The **Grosso** family practically has engine oil in their veins. For them racing represents not just a way of life but a tradition that goes back to NASCAR's inception. Like all families, they also have a few skeletons to hide. What happens when someone peeks inside the closet becomes a matter that threatens to destroy them.

The **Murphys** have been supporting drivers in the pits for generations, despite a vendetta with the Grossos that's almost as old as NASCAR itself! But the Murphys have their own secrets... and a few indiscretions that could cost them everything.

The **Branches** are newcomers, and some would say upstarts. But as this affluent Texas family is further enmeshed in the world of NASCAR, they become just as embroiled in the intrigues on and off the track.

The **Motor Media Group** are the PR people responsible for the positive public perception of NASCAR's stars. They are the glue that repairs the damage. And more than anything, they feel the brunt of the backlash....

These NASCAR families have secrets to hide, and reputations to protect. This season will test them all.

Dear Reader,

My husband and I were high school sweethearts—gymnasium dances and drive-in movies. At the tender age of fifteen he introduced me to the exciting world of auto racing. He was an automotive technician, also an avid fan of internal combustion, acceleration and NASCAR.

We grew up in Vancouver, British Columbia, mere miles from the Westwood road-racing circuit and half an hour from the Mission Raceway drag strip. He also raced autocross at an abandoned airstrip, off road in a custom-built jeep and tried ice racing on the frozen lakes of the province's interior.

So when I was asked to be part of Harlequin's officially licensed NASCAR romance series, I couldn't wait to get started. I'd watched hundreds of NASCAR races. I knew the sights, the sounds, the smells of racing. I'd been in the pits and garages, watched the green flag drop and the checkered flag wave. Thanks to my husband, this was a world I knew I could put on the page.

I loved writing *Overheated*. The memories it brought back were a bonus. I hope you enjoy!

Barbara

NASCAR

OVERHEATED

Barbara Dunlop

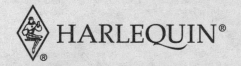

HARLEQUIN®

TORONTO • NEW YORK • LONDON
AMSTERDAM • PARIS • SYDNEY • HAMBURG
STOCKHOLM • ATHENS • TOKYO • MILAN • MADRID
PRAGUE • WARSAW • BUDAPEST • AUCKLAND

ISBN-13: 978-0-373-21792-2
ISBN-10:   0-373-21792-7

OVERHEATED

BARBARA DUNLOP

is a bestselling, award-winning author of numerous novels for Harlequin and Silhouette Books. Her books regularly hit bestseller lists for series romance, and she has twice been short-listed for the Romance Writers of America's RITA® Award.

Barbara lives in a log house in the Yukon, where the bears outnumber people, and moose graze the front yard. By day she works as the Yukon's film commissioner. By night she pens romance novels in front of a roaring fire.

For my husband

REARVIEW MIRROR:

Everyone's talking about the recent engagement
of Motor Media Group public relations spokesperson
Anita Wolcott and PDQ Racing's new owner, Jim Latimer.
But there's no gossip juicier than the romance—or rather,
the twenty-two-year age difference—between Larry Grosso
and Crystal Hayes.

CHAPTER ONE

CRYSTAL HAYES WAS GLAD OF the familiar chaos as the NASCAR Sprint Cup Series teams arrived for the race at Charlotte. The town was abuzz with activity, and the fast pace of track deliveries from Softco Machine Works kept her mind off the little things—like her bank balance.

Thursday morning, she swung the company delivery truck out the bay door of Softco's east shop. The complex had grown from its humble beginnings as a single bay garage to an impressive complex of three modern machine shops, two warehouses and a ten-person office. There was an apartment over the office, where Crystal had lived since her husband, Simon, died two years ago.

But she wasn't thinking about that today. In particular, she wasn't stressing about how long a twenty-eight-year-old woman could live above her parents' business without looking pathetic. Today, she was headed for the speedway in Charlotte and the Dean Grosso garage to be part of the pulsating hive of activity surrounding a premier NASCAR event.

She pulled the truck onto Deerborne Street and headed north toward the interstate. When she got up to speed, she popped a vintage Creedence CD into the player, in the mood to get nostalgic. Her father had played Creedence, Pink Floyd and Nazareth in the truck when Crystal was a child riding along on deliveries, and she still had a soft spot in her heart for classic rock.

She toured past the Rondal Bicycle Factory and the Pearson Furniture Warehouse before traffic increased and the landscape turned to retail businesses. The bright red, Treatsy-Sweetsy ice-cream parlor sign rotated slowly in the distance, its stylized, red *TS* towering above the surrounding buildings. Crystal could almost hear her childhood voice begging her dad to stop for a butterscotch cone.

She smiled to herself as Creedence rasped on about the calm before the storm.

She thought about the forty-odd dollars in her pocket. She'd planned to treat herself to a pizza on Saturday night, which would leave her with just enough for groceries until her next Softco paycheck. If she splurged on a cone, she'd have to compromise somewhere else.

A part-time job as a delivery driver, combined with the occasional advance check on her short stories, didn't exactly provide for a high lifestyle. But she wasn't touching Simon's military widow's pension and life insurance policy, not even to relive the childhood memory.

The rotating sign loomed closer.

She could taste the velvet smooth ice cream, the crisp waffle cone—made daily on site, as they had been for thirty years. She could feel the melting butterscotch oozing over her fingers in the hot, May sunshine.

Oh, to hell with the pizza.

She stomped on the brakes, gluing the unwieldy box of a vehicle to the hot pavement. The tires protested with a screech, but she made the corner, parked across four marked spaces in back of the lot and shut down the diesel engine.

She rounded the building and approached a small patch

of garden between the street and the front entrance. There was a black Lab tied to a spindly shrub at one edge of the sparse lawn. Somebody had brought him some water in a Treatsy-Sweetsy ice-cream bowl, but he wasn't drinking it.

He was staring off down the sidewalk, twitching at the end of his lead.

He watched one car approach, brows up, ears quirked. Then it passed without slowing, and the anticipation leeched out of his body. He moved onto the next car, growing alert, obviously expecting his owner to appear at any second. He had gray fur around his muzzle, and a chunk missing from one floppy ear, testifying to a long, probably less than pampered, life.

Crystal drew his attention, and he watched her with big, brown eyes. For a second, she was tempted to buy him a burger. But she quickly reminded herself that she was broke. She'd already compromised her Saturday night pizza. Plus, she reasoned, the owner might not appreciate random strangers feeding his dog.

The small Treatsy-Sweetsy dining room was a whole lot cooler than outside. It was also completely empty, so she walked straight up to the counter. She looked up at the menu board, debating between a regular and a large cone. She wasn't worried about the calories, only the price. She had a naturally thin frame, and a metabolism that was very forgiving of her abuses.

"Help you?" asked a young, ponytailed girl in a pink and white striped blouse and dangling white, plastic earrings.

"A large butterscotch cone."

The girl nodded and rung the price into the cash register. "Two seventy-five."

Crystal handed her a twenty and glanced back at the dog.

He was still standing at the end of the yellow rope, twitching at something he saw down the street, his expression hopeful.

"Your change," said the girl, and Crystal turned back.

"What's with the dog?" she asked.

"Animal Control's coming for him."

This surprised Crystal. For some reason, he hadn't struck her as a stray. He seemed intelligent and, well, dignified—if the word could be applied to an old dog with such a battered ear.

"Is he lost?" she asked.

The girl shook her head, jiggling her plastic earrings and swaying her ponytail. "There was a car accident this morning." She pointed. "Old man hit the tree."

Crystal stared back, seeing the white gash in a stately, old oak.

"Old guy was killed. Dog was fine."

Crystal's heart instantly went out to the poor dog, and her chest tightened painfully. His owner wouldn't be coming back. And the city pound would...

She swallowed, not allowing herself to think about what might happen at the pound.

"Did he have relatives?" asked Crystal. Maybe there were children or grandchildren who'd take the dog.

"The dog?"

"The man."

Another shrug. "Didn't know his name. Came in here alone a lot." She took a sugar cone from the stack and opened the ice cream bin.

Crystal watched the girl form a scoop of the swirled butterscotch, feeling like a heel for indulging in something as silly as ice cream when the poor dog was probably about to be put down.

It's not like somebody was likely to adopt him. The pound was full of bright, lively puppies. Who would choose an old, gray-whiskered dog with a bad ear?

The girl balled up a second scoop, while Crystal felt an impulse growing within her.

"If I give you my name," she said, half her brain telling her to shut up, the other half urging her on. "Will you tell the pound people I've got the dog?"

The girl stopped mid scoop, staring blankly at Crystal.

"I'll take care of him until they check for relatives," Crystal explained. How sad would it be if somebody put the dog down, then a relative showed up later? She knew the pound didn't keep stray animals for long.

"You're taking the dog?" the girl asked, clearly confused.

Crystal nodded. "Do you have a pen?"

The clerk seemed to remember she was in the middle of making a cone. She added the second scoop and handed the cone to Crystal. Then she pulled a pen from under the counter.

Crystal quickly jotted down her name and number on one of the Treatsy-Sweetsy napkins and handed it to the girl. "Tell them to call me if they find a relative."

The clerk nodded bemusedly, while Crystal turned for the exit, telling herself she hadn't lost her mind. There was nothing wrong with occasionally being a Good Samaritan.

Out on the hot sidewalk, she gingerly petted the dog. He sighed and gazed up at her, giving his tail only a cursory wag. But his round eyes closed while she scratched between his ears.

Okay. That was one question answered. It didn't look like he'd bite her.

Carefully balancing the melting cone, she untied the rope from the shrub and coiled a few loops around her free hand.

"There we go, doggy," she crooned. "You want to go for a car ride?"

Predictably, he didn't answer, but stared silently up at her with an expression of benevolent patience. He seemed confused when she started to walk. But after a moment, he came willingly enough.

Across the parking lot, she opened the passenger door. Again, he gave her a curious stare.

"Up you go," she prompted.

He jumped onto the floor of the truck.

Crystal patted the seat.

He gave her a look that questioned her wisdom, his brows knitting together. But when she patted it a second time, he gamely hopped up, curling into a little ball.

She shut the door, refusing to examine the logic of her actions. It was a temporary fix, just until the old man's family could be contacted. And if no relative showed up, well, she'd deal with that later.

On the way around the cab, she licked a dribble from the back of her hand, then she swiped her tongue across both scoops a few times, making her way down to the solid ice cream before hopping into the truck.

She turned the key in the ignition.

"Okay, dog," she said aloud, with a forced note of bravery in her voice. "Looks like it's you and me for a while."

She gave the dog the rest of her ice cream, then put the truck into Reverse.

RUFUS, AS CRYSTAL HAD decided to call the black Lab, slept soundly on the soft seat, even as she maneuvered the

Softco truck in front of the Dean Grosso garage. Engines fired through the open bay doors, compressors clacked and impact tools whined as the teams tweaked their race cars in preparation for qualifying.

As always, when she visited the garage area, Crystal experienced a vicarious thrill, watching the technicians' meticulous, last-minute preparations. As the daughter of a machinist, she understood the difference a fraction of a degree or a thousandth of an inch could make in the performance of a race car.

She muscled the driver's door shut behind her and waved hello to a couple of familiar team members in their white and pale-blue uniforms. Then she rounded to the back of the truck and rolled up the door. Inside, five boxes were marked Cargill Motorsports.

One of them was big and heavy; it had slid forward a few feet, probably when she'd braked to make the Treatsy-Sweetsy parking lot entrance. So she pushed up the sleeves of her canary-yellow shirt, then stretched forward to reach the box. A couple of catcalls came her way as her faded blue jeans tightened across her rear end. But she knew they were good natured, so she simply ignored them.

She dragged the box toward her, over the gritty, metal floor.

"Let me give you a hand with that," a deep, melodious voice rumbled in her ear.

"I can manage," she responded crisply, not wanting to engage with any of the cat-callers.

Here in the garage, the last thing she needed was one of the guys treating her like she was something other than, well, one of the guys.

She'd learned long ago that there was something about her that made men toss out pickup lines like parade candy.

And she'd been around race teams long enough to know she needed to behave like a buddy, not a potential date.

She piled the smaller boxes on top of the large one.

"It looks heavy," said the voice.

"I'm tough," she assured him as she scooped the pile into her arms.

He didn't move away, so she turned her head to subject him to a *back off* stare. But she found herself staring into a compelling pair of green...no, brown...no, hazel eyes. She did a double take, as they seemed to twinkle, multi-colored, under the garage lights.

The man insistently held out his hands for the boxes. There was a dignity in his tone, and little crinkles around his eyes that hinted at wisdom. There wasn't a single sign of flirtation in his expression, but Crystal was still cautious.

"You know I'm being paid to move this, right?" she asked him.

"That doesn't mean I can't be a gentleman."

Somebody whistled from a workbench. "Go, Professor Larry."

The man named Larry tossed his own back-off look over his shoulder. Then he turned to Crystal. "Sorry about that."

"Are you for real?" she asked, growing uncomfortable with the attention they were drawing. The last thing she needed was some latter-day Sir Galahad defending her honor at the track.

He quirked a dark eyebrow in a question.

"I mean," she elaborated, "you don't need to worry. I've been fending off the wolves since I was seventeen."

"Doesn't make it right," he countered, attempting to lift the box from her hands.

She jerked back. "You're not making it any easier."

He frowned.

"You carry this box, and they start thinking of me as a girl."

Professor Larry dipped his gaze to take in the curves of her figure. "Hate to tell you this," he said, a little smile coming into those multifaceted eyes. "Odds are," Larry continued, a teasing drawl in his tone, "they already have."

Something about his look make her shiver inside. It was a ridiculous reaction. Guys had given her the once-over a million times. She'd learned long ago to ignore it.

She turned pointedly away, boxes in hand as she marched across the floor. She could feel him watching her from behind.

He was just like the rest.

But then, she remembered his apology for the team member's ribald remark. She couldn't help but smile at that. When was the last time anyone cared how she felt about being the subject of sexual overtures?

"Hey, Crystal." Dean Grosso greeted her as she set the boxes down on the workbench. "I see you met my brother, Larry."

Crystal glanced back at the tall man who still stood beside her truck. Dean's brother? Really? She would have pegged Larry as much younger than Dean.

"Is he really a professor?" she asked, dusting off her hands and tucking her chestnut hair behind her ears. In the past couple of months, her hair had grown out to a nondescript style. But until she figured out her economic life, she didn't want to spend any money on a haircut. Plus, anything she could do to look plain and boring was a good thing in her world.

Crew chief Perry Noble approached, pulling a pen out of his shirt pocket.

"Applied Mathematics at State," Dean said to Crystal, while Perry signed the packing slip for the custom parts.

"He doesn't look like a nerd to me," she noted, thinking Larry looked a lot more like a businessman than a mathematician.

He appeared urbane and classy, with dark, neatly trimmed hair. He had intelligent eyes and a serious, square chin, and he wore a gray, pinstripe dress shirt and a maroon tie, with charcoal slacks and a pair of black loafers. Even without a suit jacket, he could probably stroll into any boardroom in America and look right at home.

Dean chuckled. "Get him talking about string theory, and you'll see just how nerdy he is."

"That's unlikely," said Crystal, accepting a copy of the signed packing slip from Perry. "I can barely understand trigonometry."

"Only thing I need to understand is acceleration," joked Dean.

"And chronology," his wife Patsy put in, joining the conversation. "Hi there, Crystal."

"She thinks I'm getting old," Dean said, frowning at Patsy.

"You're getting older every year," she pointed out.

"Mathematically correct," Crystal agreed.

As one of the veteran NASCAR drivers, Dean's age was a matter of public interest. Fans and commentators alike were fond of speculating about his possible retirement. His brother Larry looked to be in his early forties. Maybe ten or so years older than Crystal. Not such a big difference. He was definitely nowhere near retirement.

Then she gave herself a little shake. What did the difference in their ages matter? She'd barely been introduced to the man. He'd offered to carry her box, not take her out on Saturday night. She was getting way ahead of herself.

"Say hello to your dad for me?" asked Patsy.

"Absolutely," Crystal said, nodding.

Softco Machine Works had provided custom machining to NASCAR teams in Charlotte since before Crystal was born. Her father was friends with most of the NASCAR families.

She gave Dean and Patsy a cheery wave goodbye as she headed back to the van.

Larry was in the bay's doorway, talking to a red-shirted race official. Crystal grabbed the rope on the rear rollup door. She caught herself in time to keep from tugging it down too quickly. She didn't want the clattering metal to scare Rufus.

As the door lowered into place, she caught Larry's movement in her peripheral vision. She gave him a wave goodbye. He smiled and nodded, and she felt an unaccustomed pull toward him.

Strange. She rarely had a desire to prolong a conversation with a man. It inevitably became complicated and uncomfortable. It didn't seem to matter how plain her clothes, or how understated her makeup and hair, she had to remain on guard for leering looks and blatant sexual innuendo. Her late husband had treated her like a sex object and she would never let that happen again.

Ignoring the urge to move in Larry's direction, she secured the door latch and strode back to the cab and Rufus.

The dog lifted his head to blink at her as she clambered back into the high seat, but he immediately settled down again. She supposed the comfort of the truck seat, along with his three-quarters of the large butterscotch cone, were enough to keep him sleepy and content for the moment.

She pushed the truck into gear, refusing to glance in the rearview mirror for a final glimpse of Professor Larry.

STRETCHING OUT HIS STROKE, Larry made a beeline down one of the fast lanes at the Northstar Recreation Center's pool. He touched the wall, did an underwater turn and counted fifty in his mind, the blue lane buoys a blur beside him. He was halfway through his workout, had burned approximately four-hundred calories, and had compensated for five hours of sedentary, computer time on his major muscle groups. He made a mental note to check the wall clock on his next turnaround to make sure he was on pace.

When his fingertips brushed the painted concrete at the shallow end of the pool, he glanced up. His view of the clock was blocked by a pair of tanned legs—female legs that curved into smooth hips and a snug, ocean-blue one-piece bathing suit.

"Hello, Larry," came a voice that triggered something primal in his nervous system.

Facts and figures fled from his brain as he craned his neck to look up at…the woman from the garage. Crystal Hayes, his brother had told him.

His vocal chords didn't immediately form words.

Her brow furrowed. "Do you remember me?"

Did he *remember* her? Hell, yes. He'd dreamed about her last night, spent most of this morning reliving their short conversation, cursing the fact that he was so formal around women, that he couldn't carry on an easy, bantering chitchat like most men could.

He'd also cursed the fact that he'd offended her by offering to carry her package. He'd wondered if she was still annoyed with him. He'd also wondered if she'd caught on to the fact that he considered her one of the most beautiful women he'd ever seen.

Which was a totally inappropriate thought, and one he'd fought hard against.

"From yesterday?" she prompted into his silence. "At the garage?"

"Yes," he blurted out.

And then she smiled. "Oh, good."

He smiled in return, searching his brain for something intelligent to say.

Imagine, a tenured professor, published in the *American Mathematics Journal* and *Quantum International,* a NASA consultant, and he couldn't think of a single intelligent thing to say to a beautiful woman.

The large pool facility was almost eerily quiet for 2:00 p.m., save for a couple of swimmers splashing a few lanes down.

"Strange that I've never seen you here before," said Crystal. Her gaze took in his arms, chest and shoulders, apparently concluding it wasn't the first time he'd been swimming.

Okay, his ego could handle that.

"I usually work out in the pool at State," he said, grateful he hadn't completely lost the power of speech.

"Your brother said you were a professor?"

Larry nodded. *Words, man. Words!*

"I teach mathematics."

"Interesting."

"That's not what most people say." Most people's eyes glazed over at the mention of his profession.

She grinned, and something about her smile warmed him inside.

"You here to do laps?" he asked.

"Three times a week."

"You can burn up to eight hundred excess calories doing an hour of freestyle."

She glanced down at herself.

He cringed. "Not that I'm suggesting… That is, of course, *you* don't need to worry about burning excess calories."

She chuckled at his horrible faux pas. "Trust me. I do it to feel good. I couldn't care less about the visual pleasure of others."

She moved to the next lane and sat down, dangling her feet and calves in the water.

Larry noticed that she was providing him with all kinds of visual pleasure at the moment, from the curve of her tanned hip, to her nipped-in waist, to the hint of cleavage. Visual pleasure didn't get much better than this.

"Guess I'd better get going," she said, slipping into the water.

"And I'd better get back at it." He'd never stopped in the middle of a workout before. It simply wasn't a logical thing to do. He quickly decided he'd better add a few laps to get his pulse rate back to optimal.

"See you later," she called, pushing off the wall, arms curling, legs scissoring, gorgeous derriere poking out of the water.

Larry cursed between clenched teeth. The woman's derriere was absolutely none of his business. He stretched into his own length, deciding three extra laps would do it.

He arrived at the far wall of the pool and was surprised to discover he hadn't passed Crystal. Logic told him to stick to his own pace, but his ego urged him to swim a little harder. In a rare move, his brain let emotion override logic.

But at the end of the next lap, she was still ahead.

He pushed harder, determined to catch her.

Five more laps, and they were even at the turn.

She flashed him a smile that said she was onto him then pushed hard off the wall, obviously prepared to give it all she had. They moved neck and neck the entire length, both laughing when they reached the wall.

"How many've you got to go?" she gasped.

"Forty-five," he responded.

"Might want to pace yourself," she suggested.

"What about you?"

A competitive gleam grew in her green eyes. "Looks like we tied in the sprint. I'll race you again for distance."

"Forty-five laps?" he asked.

She nodded toward the scattered tables of the on-deck snack bar. "Loser buys fruit smoothies."

"You're on."

Larry pushed off with determination.

At ten laps, he was surprised by her strength.

By twenty laps, he realized she must have done a whole lot of swimming in her life.

By thirty laps, he began to fear she might actually beat him.

But by forty laps, her speed began to slow.

He drew a deep breath of relief. He could have kept up the pace right to the end, but he might not have been able to walk afterward. He let himself slow down with her, and touched the final wall mere inches ahead of her.

She smoothed back her slick, dark hair, smiling brightly at him, looking like something out of a fantasy movie. "You're very good," she acknowledged.

"What about you? I take it you've done some swimming in your time?"

"Wesleyan College swim team."

"You telling me I've been hustled?"

"Fork over the smoothie, baby."

"I'd call it a tie." He was prepared to be gracious.

She placed her palms on the pool deck, slipping her slick body out of the water. "Photo finish, but I won."

"You sure?"

"I'm positive."

He laughed and gave it to her, resting his gaze on her clinging swimsuit. Fact was, he'd buy her a hundred smoothies, or anything else she wanted, no race necessary.

He hopped out of the pool beside her. She was taller than most women. He had maybe four inches on her, and he couldn't help thinking she was the perfect height.

"Do I get a rematch?" he asked.

"Not today." She made a show of stretching out her arm muscles.

He smiled at that. He didn't have a rematch in him today, either.

They strolled across the deck in silence, stopping at the bank of lockers for their towels.

Larry draped his around his shoulders and retrieved his wallet. "You live in Charlotte?"

She nodded, rubbing her towel over her hair before securing it at her waist. "I grew up here. Funny that we've never met before."

"I don't spend a lot of time in the garage." When he came to a race, he was often in a motor home or up top with his son Steve who spotted for his nephew Kent, another NASCAR Sprint Cup Series driver.

"And I'm usually somewhere else," she said, as they headed for the all-weather carpet and white plastic deck furniture of the snack bar.

"Do you watch the races at all?"

"If I'm at my parents' house, yeah. My dad hasn't missed one in about thirty years."

"But you don't come out to watch at the track?"

She shrugged. "Occasionally."

They crossed into the snack bar where a dozen tables were clustered in an atrium. About half were full of families or couples.

"Ever seen a race from the pits?"

"You mean a hot pass?" She stopped beside the semi-circular counter and gazed up at the painted menu.

"A hot pass," he confirmed. The pits during a race had to be experienced to be believed.

"Never had one of those."

It was on the tip of Larry's tongue to make the offer. She was obviously cleared through track security for her job. He could get her a hot pass for Sunday, and they could watch the cars thunder down the straightaway together. But it would be almost like asking her on a date. And he was pretty sure that was inappropriate.

"I'll take a strawberry-banana," she said to a teenage clerk with short, streaked hair and a silver ring through her eyebrow.

Just like that, the moment was lost.

"Pineapple-mango," said Larry, dropping his credit card on the green Arborite.

"I guess you have access to everything behind the scenes," she said.

There it was again, another opportunity to invite her to the track. "Some things," he said, wondering if he could phrase it in a way that didn't make it sound like he was coming on to her. He could invite her to meet the family—his brother Dean, son Steve and nephew Ken. Would that make it better or worse?

The whine of the blender filled the air.

"Do you like racing?" she asked.

"I love it," he answered honestly.

"But you're not involved?"

"I love it as a spectator and a fan. But I'm not mechanically inclined, and I'm definitely not a driver." Larry had learned a long time ago that his brain liked concepts better than hands-on. He might be able to help design a racing engine, but somebody else had to put it together.

Crystal looked him up and down. "You'd look cute in one of those uniforms."

Even though he wasn't crazy about the "cute" adjective, his breath caught again on her smile. "I have absolutely no desire to go 180 miles an hour. My family knew early on I'd never be a driver."

Then he rethought the burst of honesty. Did it make him sound timid? Nerdy?

The clerk slid the smoothies across the counter, and Larry signed the credit card slip.

"I'd try it once," said Crystal, capturing the plastic straw between her white teeth. "Just to see what it felt like."

Larry's gaze caught on her red lips as they wrapped around the straw and took a pull on the thick drink.

Then she grinned. "Of course, there's every chance I'd scream my head off."

She stirred the straw through the drink as she turned away. He watched her long legs, the sway of her hips, and the smooth skin of her bare shoulders. She was gorgeous enough to be on a Paris runway. And for the first time since his wife died three years ago, Larry felt a rush of sexual desire.

He tore his gaze from her body, scooped the other smoothie from the countertop, and followed her.

Crystal chose a corner table between a potted fig and a glass wall that overlooked the park. The ceiling was lower here than in the pool area, dampening the echoes of the growing swim crowd.

Larry rushed forward to help with her chair, and she turned to give him a bemused smiled. "Thanks."

"You're welcome." He took the chair opposite, setting his drink on the table.

"So, you bucked the family business," she began, dabbing her straw up and down.

"I did," he agreed, struggling to keep his gaze from straying below her neck.

"Were they disappointed?"

"That I became a professor instead of a mechanic?"

She tipped her head sideways. "It sounds strange when you say it that way."

"Only to people who don't understand the value of a good mechanic."

"And you do?"

"I became a professor, because I'd make a lousy mechanic."

"And I became a parts driver, because I made a lousy model."

"You were a model?" It didn't surprise him.

"For a couple of months. I hated it."

He raised his eyebrows, waiting for her to continue.

"The sum total of your being is reduced to the size of your waist and the length of your legs."

He couldn't help it, his gaze dipped down. Luckily, she didn't notice.

She wiggled forward in her chair. "I felt like some kind of a mechanical Barbie doll. Face this way. Walk that way. Frown, pout, stare. And all those people." She shuddered.

"Ogling you. They pretend it's about the clothes, but half of them are checking out your body."

"Why did you try it in the first place?"

"I was in college, and the money was good."

"What was your major?" he asked, feeling himself relax in a way he rarely did around women.

"Creative writing, plus some history and anthropology."

"But you became a parts driver?"

"Unlike you, I didn't buck the family business."

He nodded, remembering the logo on the side of her van. "Softco Machine Works."

"Mom and Dad are good for a paycheck."

"Do you write at all?" He knew it was tough to make a living as a writer.

She nodded, sliding her fingertip through the condensation on her glass. Larry had to remind himself to take a drink of his own melting concoction.

"Short stories mostly, based on the lives of the women who settled the South. That's why I like driving for Softco. It's part-time, and the hours are flexible. If I'm working on a story, I can come in late or take off early."

"That sounds fascinating," he told her honestly.

"Mostly it's traffic lights and getting cut off by sports cars."

"You know what I meant."

"It's fascinating," she agreed. "Particularly the interviews. And I'm working on a cookbook and anthology that my publisher thinks might pay off."

"Tell me about it." Larry took a long pull on the pineapple-mango smoothie, wondering how he could possibly segue from a cookbook to a date.

CHAPTER TWO

ON SUNDAY MORNING, CRYSTAL had to settle for bran cereal instead of cold, leftover pepperoni pizza. On the bright side, she now had a dozen cans of dog food, a shiny black dog dish and a leather leash dangling from one of the hooks beside her kitchen door. On the down side, she might have to ask her mother for an advance this week.

Rufus was curled up, asleep on the woven mat in front of the fireplace. It would have been a picture-perfect scene, if the fireplace had worked, if it wasn't ninety degrees outside and if Rufus hadn't snored like a longshoreman. The dog had remained aloof for the past two days. He was polite, but clearly confused, and he still had an air of watchfulness and waiting about him.

The phone rang, and he jumped to his feet.

"It won't be for you, boy," she said, then added, "Sorry."

Still, he watched her closely while she crossed the faded, yellow linoleum to retrieve the cordless phone from the top of the washing machine. The readout showed it was her mother from downstairs in the office.

She clicked the talk button. "Hey, Mom."

The computerized lathes and milling machines rumbled in the background. "Are you up?" called Stella Hayes.

"I've been up for an hour," said Crystal. It was way too hot to sleep late.

"Good. Norman's been up since four this morning ma-chining a backup axle for Dean Grosso, just in case, and we need a delivery driver."

Crystal experienced a moment's hesitation.

The Dean Grosso garage might bring her into contact with Larry again. Not that that was a bad thing. It was simply a…strange thing.

There was something about the man that made her restless and edgy, not to mention uncharacteristically ex-pansive. When she thought back over their conversation, she couldn't believe how much she'd rattled on about her Colonial cookbook and anthology project.

She also couldn't believe a man who was helping the world explore the asteroid belt had been interested in her writing project. Looking back, she worried that he'd simply been humoring her.

When she'd asked, he'd admitted he was consulting on an ion propulsion engine for NASA. Although most of the technicalities escaped her, Larry explained how a blue beam of light that could barely push a piece of paper on earth could eventually propel a spaceship to thousands of miles an hour. The man was a bona fide rocket scientist.

"Crystal?" her mother prompted.

"Sorry, Mom."

Rufus gave up and went back to the mat.

"Can you drive today?"

"Sure." Everybody pitched in during race week. Besides, Stella was as practical and no-nonsense as they came. Crystal could hardly explain that she didn't want to go because she got a funny feeling from a man who might be at the track.

"Give me fifteen minutes?" asked Crystal.

"The axle will be ready when you are."

Crystal set down the phone and gazed at Rufus. She'd taken him for a walk first thing this morning. But for some reason, he hadn't seemed able to find the right spot to do his business. She didn't dare leave him inside or load him into the truck without walking him now.

She slipped into a pair of running shoes and retrieved the leash.

"Walk, Rufus?" she asked.

His uneven ears perked up.

She jingled the leash.

He came to his feet, looking at least a little bit interested in the activity as he padded toward her.

"Good for you," she crooned, scratching him on the head as she clipped onto his worn, leather collar

She scooped her purse from the counter, popped a cap on her head, then locked up behind her.

She led him down the long staircase to the paved parking lot behind the office. They crossed to the wooded area out back, taking the trail that skirted Stanley Pond.

Happily, as soon as she let him off the leash, Rufus got right down to business.

Afterward, she clipped him back on and took the long way around to the bay door and the delivery truck. She might be committed to temporarily fostering Rufus, but her mother would find a dog entirely impractical. And Crystal wasn't ready to have that argument just yet.

So she hustled him into the passenger seat and shut the door before tracking down the shop foreman to get the paperwork for the delivery.

While she drove, she tried not to think about whether Larry would be at his brother's garage. He'd said he didn't spend much time down there. And, really, it was of little consequence.

He was a nice guy, sure. And they'd had a fun chat over smoothies. She was impressed by his intellect and, she'd admit, she kind of liked his formal, courteous manner.

The man had actually pulled out her chair. She smiled at the memory. Even more impressive, they'd carried on an hour-long conversation. She couldn't remember the last time a man had shown such a strong interest in her thoughts and ideas. Simon never had.

Which meant she was probably hanging out with the wrong kind of men. Something to think about for the future.

She swung north on I-85, glancing at her watch, thinking maybe she'd try to stay at the track for the race. There was no law that said she had to watch it from her parents' living room. She could buy a ticket for the grandstands, or maybe she could wrangle a pit pass, and maybe she'd meet up with Larry again.

She made up her mind. If Larry was there, she'd ask him to get her a pit pass.

The odds of her running into him amidst the two-hundred odd thousand spectators was slim. But, if lightning did strike twice, she promised herself she'd ask. Maybe they'd chat some more. Maybe she'd figure out what it was she was supposed to be feeling about him.

At the track, she carefully maneuvered between haulers, service vehicles and hundreds of people rushing to get ready for the race. The noise level was high, the excitement level even higher.

She squeezed the delivery truck as close as she could get to the Cargill Motorsports garage and lined the back of the truck up with the bay door. Before shutting off the motor, she lowered both windows to give Rufus some fresh air.

He yawned and stretched, finding a more comfortable position on the seat, his ears flopping over the edge. She gave him a scratch on the head, and a sigh whooshed through his body.

"You have a dog," came a familiar male voice through her open window.

She turned to find herself face-to-face with Larry, his eyes taking on a green tone in the bright sunlight.

Something lurched in her chest, and she went breathless. "I'm fostering him," she managed.

"I've never had a dog," said Larry.

"My first," she admitted. Her parents always claimed to be too busy for a pet. The business came first. Running Softco Machine Works took sixteen-hour days, seven days a week.

Larry opened the truck door for her, and Crystal slipped off the seat, her running shoes coming down onto the roasting pavement.

"And here you are again," she observed as they both headed down the length of the delivery truck.

"Surprised?" he asked.

"I'm surprised you're in the garage twice in a row."

"Yeah." His expression sobered. "After the incident with Kent's car—"

"Those animal-right activists?" Crystal had heard about the incident on the radio.

"I thought the family might need some moral support."

She nodded, admiring his devotion to his family. It was nice of him to show up to lend a hand.

She flipped the latch and rolled up the door. "And here all I brought was an axle."

"That's important, too." He gazed at the boxes in the depths of the truck. "Any chance you'll let me carry the box?"

"You're treating me like a girl again."

"I know," he agreed. There was a thickness in the inflection of his voice.

She looked up, and there it was. A wave of desire sizzled between them. She could almost smell the scorched heat. Although she supposed it could have been tire smoke.

"Can you get me a pit pass?" she asked, partly because she'd promised herself she would and partly because this feeling was very much worth investigating.

His eyes registered surprise. "Sure."

"Good." She lifted the long box. "Then go do that while I finish up here."

His gaze flicked to the box, and she could see the war going on inside him.

"Don't even think about it," she warned.

"Is it more than ten pounds?"

"None of your business." It was probably about forty. "I do this for a living, remember?"

"You write for a living," he countered.

"If I only wrote for a living, I'd be residing in a cardboard box and be a whole lot thinner than I already am."

He took in her figure beneath the khaki pants and plain T-shirt. He didn't say a word, but his expression told her he liked what he saw.

She liked that he liked it, which was not her normal reaction.

"You going to let me stand here holding this box?" she asked.

He reflexively reached for it.

"I meant you should get out of my way."

He stepped to one side to give her the room she needed. "Sorry."

But she grinned. "Don't be sorry. Please go get me a pit pass."

Larry gave her a salute and a smile in return, as he turned to go.

"I'll park Rufus in the shade," she called after him. "And get him some water."

Larry turned back and shot her a grimace. "His name is really Rufus?"

"I picked it myself. You got a problem with that?"

He held up his hands in surrender. "No problem here."

She shifted her attention to the garage to find the Grosso team watching with bemused expressions on their faces.

"My new dog," Crystal explained as she walked toward the workbench, pretending what she and Larry had going was nothing more than a budding acquaintance. And it *wasn't* anything more than that—despite the flutters of anticipation gathering in her stomach.

THERE WAS TROUBLE ON THE track.

There was also trouble on pit road.

Out on Turn Three, race cars banged into each other like dominos. Metal clanged, tires screeched and smoke filled the early evening air. Near the Kent Grosso pit box, Crystal's hand clamped down on Larry's knee. The yellow caution flag came out, while the warning flags inside Larry's head turned to red.

He nearly gasped out loud as sensation zapped up his thigh at the speed of light. Okay, it was more like the speed of his circulatory system, or more appropriately, the speed of synaptic transmission along his sympathetic nervous system.

Okay, forget the science.

Her hand was on his knee.

Then Steve's voice filled his headset, warning Kent to go high. Larry's mathematical mind automatically kicked in, calculating the spinning cars' trajectory, and he knew his son's advice was right.

Then suddenly, Justin Murphy shot to the outside. Steve's frantic warning came too late, and Kent lost control.

Crystal's delicate fingers squeezed tight. Since Larry knew the likely g-forces and the capability of the safety equipment, he wasn't concerned about his nephew as the car spun into the infield, where it rolled once, landing upright.

The knowledge left him free to focus on Crystal's squeeze. What did it mean? What should he do? More important, had anyone noticed?

He glanced at the team members around them, but everyone's attention was on Kent's car. The engine fired again, shooting smoke out the tailpipe, and the crew breathed a collective sigh of relief. Then Kent was pulling from the infield onto the track.

The crash was disappointing for his son, Steve, and the rest of the Maximus Motorsports team. But that was racing. There'd be another chance to climb in the standings next weekend.

Larry's attention went back to Crystal. He gazed at her long, feminine fingers, then twisted his head to catch her profile, trying to figure out if she was even aware of the touch.

His family was having a hell of a day, but all he could think of was Crystal.

She smiled at him. "That was a relief," she shouted over the throbbing noise of the pits. And her attention went back to the No. 427 car. She patted Larry's knee twice before removing her hand.

"A relief," he managed to force out.

If he'd been in a movie theatre—and ten years younger—he might have put an arm along the back of her chair. And she might have rested her head on his shoulder. He could have smelled her perfume, maybe taken her hand, maybe even kissed her there in the dark.

But he wasn't ten years younger. And it sure wasn't dark. Millions of watts of light beat down on the track, and thousands of cheering people surrounded them. Larry was personal friends with an astonishing number of those thousands of people; they were sure to ask what he thought he was doing, if he showed any kind of physical affection toward a women who looked closer to his son's age than his own.

And then there was Elizabeth, Libby.

Larry hadn't felt an attraction to any woman since his wife had died three years ago. He felt a little guilty. A few days ago he had placed flowers on her grave.

Libby was a warm glow inside his heart, and she'd always be there. But Crystal was…vibrant. And, Lord help him, he was ready to move on.

She applauded Kent's signal to the fans that he was okay, pointing to her headset and nodding her approval to indicate she understood how frustrated Steve must be because he wasn't able to stop Justin from knocking Kent out. She patted Larry's shoulder, smiled and nodded. He thought she was saying he should be proud of his son's contribution.

He *was* proud. Of his son. Of his wife. Of the wonderful life they'd had as a family. But Libby was gone now, and Steve was all grown up, and Larry was alone.

And he didn't want to be alone today. He wanted to be with Crystal. And whatever these feelings were for her, he didn't want them to stop just yet.

He leaned over, lifting one side of her headset to shout above the noise. "You want to do dinner after this?"

It would be a little late by the time the race wrapped up, but so far today neither of them had eaten at the track.

She leaned close to yell into his free ear. "I have to take Rufus home and drop off the truck."

He wasn't sure if the reason was bona fide, or if she was giving him a polite brush off.

"Tuesday?" he forced himself to ask. If he was getting shot down, it might as well be quick and thorough.

"Tuesday's good," she said, nodding.

Larry couldn't stop the wide grin that grew on his face. "Rouladen's?" he suggested, naming his favorite restaurant.

She cringed at the name of the expensive establishment.

He hesitated a second. Was she uncomfortable with such a romantic atmosphere? Did she think he'd have expectations later?

He lifted her headset once more and leaned in. "Unless you'd prefer something different."

"It's just that I'm between paychecks," she admitted.

He drew back, offended. "You're my guest!"

"It's not 1950."

He gave a snort of disgust. "I don't care if it's 2050, you're still my guest."

She nudged him with her shoulder. "You're an old-fashioned guy, huh?"

"For the record, I grew up in the seventies, the bastion of women's liberation. But you're still my guest."

That got a smile out of her. "Then I guess I'll try to find something suitable to wear."

"Wear anything you'd like." Crystal could show up in a bathrobe for all he cared.

TUESDAY NIGHT, RUFUS wandered into the bedroom while Crystal rifled through her meager wardrobe. He curled up on the floor to watch, at the foot of her queen-size bed, next to the old rocking chair she'd pilfered from her parents' basement.

He gave the room a cozy feeling, and she realized she was starting to enjoy the company.

"The red or the blue?" she asked him, holding up a slinky red satin-and-sequin number she hadn't worn in two years, next to a simpler, ice-blue silk dress that was one of her favorites.

Rufus lifted his nose to sniff the air, seeming to consider each of the dresses in turn.

The red was guaranteed to turn heads, and it should make Larry see her in a whole new light.

Was that what she wanted?

She held it in front of her and turned to the mirror.

Did she want to flirt with Larry? Did she want him thinking of her as sexy? She cringed at her reflection and groaned out loud.

What was she thinking? One of the things she liked best about Larry was that he saw her as a whole person, not simply as a sex object. Why would she do anything to change that?

Because she wanted him to make a move, she admitted to herself. And that was sadly hypocritical. He was one of the few men in her life who weren't trying to get her into bed, and she was planning to vamp him with red satin.

She tossed the red dress on the bed.

"The blue," she said to Rufus, holding it up in front of the mirror. "It's comfortable and classy, and it'll help me blend." She gave herself a decisive nod then headed for the bathroom.

A shower, a blow dry and a judicious makeup application later, she slipped into the dress and clipped some aquamarine earrings in her ears. She paired them up with a plain silver chain and decided that her inexpensive watch was a close-enough match. She was heading for the bedroom closet to pick some shoes, when the phone rang.

Rufus followed as she padded to the living room.

"Hello?"

"Crystal?" It was her sister Amber's voice, its tone high with excitement.

"What's going on?" asked Crystal, glancing at the clock on the wall. It was nearly seven. She didn't have a lot of time to chat.

"Zane called," Amber said breathlessly.

"Oh, no," Crystal immediately groaned. Amber's ex-husband was never good news. When he blew into town, he was either drunk or wanted money, usually both.

"No, it's good," Amber insisted.

Crystal paused, her voice turning cautious. "What do you mean good?"

"He's doing better."

"Amber—"

"He wants to talk, Crystal. And I want to talk to him. He says he hasn't had a drink in—"

"Stop right there." Crystal plunked down on her couch.

"All we're going to do is *talk*."

"You know what happened last time you talked." The last time Zane showed up, claiming he was a changed man and wanted to try again, he and Amber had partied hard. It took all of two weeks for the weasel to run through Amber's savings account and break her heart again.

Amber's voice hardened. "You never did like him."

"It's not a matter of liking or disliking." It was a matter of decent versus dysfunctional.

"It's not like there are thousands of men out there."

"Actually, there are. Hundreds of thousands in North Carolina alone. Many of them good ones."

"Zane's a good one."

Crystal sighed. They'd had this argument many times. "You're beautiful, Amber."

"No, *you're* beautiful." Amber nearly wailed. "You don't know what it's like."

"I know what Zane's like."

"He's a decent man, and a good father."

"Don't tell me he wants to see the kids." Now Crystal was really worried.

"No," Amber sniffed, and Crystal could hear the pout in her voice. "Not at the moment. He wants to see me. But I can't go meet him without a babysitter."

Crystal closed her eyes. Bingo. The reason for the call. "I can't."

"Why not? Just for a little while. You and the kids can have mac and cheese for dinner."

"I have a—" Okay, it wasn't really a date. "I'm going out."

"Where?"

"None of your business."

"Well, it can't be more important than my marriage."

"You don't have a marriage. You have a loser of a—"

"*You* stop right there."

Crystal took a breath.

"Zane may not be perfect," said Amber. "But he was my husband, and he is trying."

Crystal clenched her teeth. Zane was not trying. Zane was a loser lounge lizard who only showed up to mooch money, then left her sister in emotional tatters.

"I can't babysit," Crystal reiterated.

"Then I'll have to think of something else." Amber's voice turned searching. "Jennifer is almost—"

"Jennifer is nine." Crystal instantly saw where this was leading. "You can't leave the kids alone, Amber."

"She's very responsible."

"No. It's illegal."

Silence. Then an airy, "I guess I'll think of something."

Damn it. Crystal knew she couldn't take the chance.

Their parents were rarely an option. If they weren't working, they were sleeping, and they tended to subject Amber to lifestyle lectures if she was doing something other than visiting the local library. Amber wouldn't call them.

If Zane showed up at the door, Amber might talk herself into leaving the children alone. Or worse, Zane might start the party right there in the apartment.

"I'll come and get them," said Crystal.

"Oh, thank you, thank you, thank you!" Amber enthused. "You're the best sister ever."

Crystal didn't agree. A good sister would have been able to talk Amber out of this insanity. She wouldn't have become an enabler.

"I'll be there in half an hour," she told Amber, punching the end button in disgust.

Crystal blew out a sigh of frustration, then dialed Larry's cell phone.

"Larry Grosso," came his crisp greeting. The sound of traffic was in the background, which meant he was already on his way. She felt terrible.

"Larry, it's Crystal."

His tone changed, becoming warm and friendly. "Hey, Crystal."

Her body hummed in reaction to the deep baritone.

She took a breath to combat the sensation. Nothing to do but blurt out the bad news. "I'm afraid I can't meet you tonight."

There was a silence.

"Larry?"

"I understand." His tone was cool.

"How can you understand? I didn't even tell you why."

"If you've changed your mind—"

"I haven't changed my mind." Good grief, she'd been looking forward to this dinner for twenty-four hours. She wasn't some flighty young thing who'd blow him off for a better offer. "My sister called. And, well, it's complicated, but I have to babysit her kids."

"I see." He obviously didn't believe her.

"It's not an excuse," she insisted. "It was a…kind of…emergency." Emergency stupidity? Was there such a thing?

"How old are the kids?" asked Larry, his tone mellowing ever so slightly.

"Jennifer's nine and David is seven."

"We can bring them along."

"To Rouladen's?"

"Well, obviously not to Rouladen's. What about Pizza Heaven?"

Something warmed in Crystal's chest. "You'd take me to Pizza Heaven?"

"Sure."

"With two kids in tow?"

"The kids would be the one and only reason to pick Pizza Heaven."

Crystal laughed. "You mean you don't want to play Bop-the-Mole or jump around in the ball room?"

There was a pause on Larry's end of the phone. "I want to hang out with you. I don't much care where we do it."

Her heart warmed some more. "You're a very nice man, Larry."

Another pause. "Well, thanks for that. I'll be there in five minutes."

"I'm going to have to change," she warned him.

"Oh, no you don't. If I'm showing up at Pizza Heaven in a suit, you're wearing whatever it is you've got on."

Crystal glanced down at the shimmering blue dress. "Well, thank goodness I didn't go with the red."

"The red?" he asked, interest clear in his tone.

"It's a little flamboyant."

"Yeah?"

"Guaranteed to turn heads."

"Put it on."

"I'm not going to put it on for Pizza Heaven." But another buzz went through Crystal's body.

Were they flirting? This definitely felt like flirting. Which was okay with her.

His tone went low. "Put it on for me."

She was tempted. She was honestly tempted to do just that.

CHAPTER THREE

JENNIFER AND DAVID ORDERED kid's combos that came with a soft drink and an ice-cream sundae, while Crystal and Larry split a pepperoni pizza and went with the beer that was on tap. Although she'd stuck with the blue dress, they'd drawn a few looks on their way in. But then Larry had slipped off his jacket and rolled up his sleeves, and now they blended somewhat with the crowd of young families.

Crystal was impressed with Larry's relaxed manner around the children.

Once David had discovered Larry consulted on the space shuttle program, Larry became his new hero. He'd peppered Larry with questions all through dinner. Even Jennifer seemed impressed.

David announced he was going to be an astronaut, and Jennifer allowed that some things about math were cool.

As the meal wound down, Larry nodded to the display board above the counter. "Can anybody tell me which price is the best deal for games tokens?"

Jennifer and David quickly swiveled on their wooden bench seat, studying the numbers. Tokens were four for a dollar, nine for two dollars, twenty-five for five dollars, and fifty-five for ten dollars.

David peered hard, then looked to Jennifer.

"Fifty-five for ten dollars," she sang out.

"Fifty-five for ten dollars," David gamely echoed.

Larry handed Jennifer a ten dollar bill. "For ten dollars, how many will you each get?"

Both the children's eyes went wide as they stared at the bill.

Jennifer bit her bottom lip. "Twenty-seven," she said. Then she grinned at Larry. "And you can have the extra one."

He smiled back. "Good answer."

The kids looked to Crystal for permission. "Go ahead and have fun," she told them.

They instantly scampered away.

"That was very nice of you," she said to Larry.

He took a sip of his beer. "I wish you'd quit calling me nice."

"You are nice."

"Nice is boring."

"You're not boring. You helped with the space shuttle."

"That seemed to impress the kids more than it impressed you."

Crystal leaned an elbow on the table and rested her chin against her hand, gazing up at him with a grin. "Go figure."

"Yeah? What would it take to impress you?"

"Rouladen's would have done it."

"Tomorrow night?" he asked without skipping a beat.

Crystal came upright, feeling guilty. "I wasn't fishing."

"I know you weren't."

"You can't buy me dinner two nights in a row."

He lifted the corner of their leftover piece of pizza. "This wasn't exactly dinner."

She waved a dismissive hand. "It was fine."

"You liked it?"

"The beer was cold, the pizza hot, and the cheese was…almost real."

"Rouladen's will have real cheese."

"You don't have—"

He took her hand in his, and she immediately stopped talking. He looked deep into her eyes. "I *want* to."

She gazed back. His grip felt good. His hand was warm and broad and strong, with thick skin and the odd callus. It didn't feel remotely like a professor's hand.

"I want to, too," she admitted.

He gave her a slow smile.

She lifted her beer mug with her free hand, leaving the other just where it was.

David shrieked, drawing her attention to where he and Jennifer were playing Bop-the-Mole.

"So, what was the emergency?" Larry asked in a low voice.

Crystal sighed heavily, keeping her gaze on the children. "My sister's ex-husband is in town," she grumbled.

"Trouble?" guessed Larry.

"Zane is always trouble. From the minute my sister laid eyes on him. To the day he got her pregnant. To the day he walked out and left her with a stack of bills and two tiny children."

"Why is he back now?"

Crystal had wondered about that. "I don't know yet."

"Does he want his kids?"

She turned her attention to Larry. "Zane couldn't care less about his kids. He's a drunk and a mooch, and he's after any money he can wring out of Amber. Then he'll walk away, breaking her heart all over again."

Larry frowned. "Sounds like a prince. Why doesn't she tell him to take a hike?"

Crystal shrugged. "Self-esteem issues. He tells her he loves her. Makes wild promises about get-rich schemes and the fabulous life they're going to lead together."

"Let me guess. You tried to talk her out of seeing him tonight?"

"You bet your ass I tried to talk her out of it."

Larry looked like he might launch into a lecture. But then the tension went out of his shoulders. "You know, you can't literally bet your ass."

The statement surprised her. She'd expected something along the lines of not being her sister's keeper.

"You got something against metaphors?"

"I mean," he continued. "What would it be worth? One ass is a hundred dollars? A thousand dollars?"

"This is the math nerd in you coming out, isn't it?"

"Now your ass," he said, leaning back to gaze down her silk dress. "That'd be worth about a million."

She gave him a mock incredulous look. "Did you seriously just offer me a million dollars for…"

His face fell. "I didn't—I mean, I wouldn't—"

She struggled to keep her face straight. "What? You don't think I'm worth it?"

He gave her a hard stare. "I'm getting the hell out of this conversation."

"You're a smart man."

"That's what my IQ results say."

"How high?"

Looking embarrassed, he gazed down at his empty beer mug. "I'm not about to tell you that."

"Why not?" she pressed. "Afraid I'll be intimidated?"

"I just don't like to talk about it. Hey, David," he called across the room. "How're you guys doing?"

The kids held up fists full of bright orange tickets

they'd won at the game and that could be redeemed for various prizes.

"Nice try," said Crystal.

"Looks like they can get a rubber gecko. Or maybe the mini fire engine."

"How high?"

Larry gave a long-suffering sigh. "You're not going to drop it, are you?"

"Not a chance."

"That would be the courteous and respectful thing to do."

"Who ever told you I was courteous and respectful? Come on, Larry. How bad can it be? I already know you're a rocket scientist."

"One sixty-five," he finally admitted.

Crystal whistled low. "That's pretty bad."

"See?"

"I mean." She put a combination of reverence and awe into her voice. "How can I ever dare talk to you again? What if I say something profoundly stupid?"

"You're not going to—"

"You must know *everything*. You must laugh at us regular folks. You must be, on all counts, a superior human being to me or anyone else on the planet."

He glared at her.

She faltered for a split second. "You do know I'm messing with you, right?"

His expression didn't change. "You mock my intellect?"

She scoffed, fairly sure now that he was messing right back. "One sixty-five. Big deal. I've got an ass that's worth a million bucks."

He tried again, but this time he couldn't completely contain his grin. "People *never* mock my intellect."

"Really? Well, it's about time somebody did."

"Larry," Jennifer shouted breathlessly, clambering back up on the bench and dumping a pile of tickets on the table. "Will you help us figure out what we can get?"

David was right behind, adding his own fistfuls of tickets to the pile.

"See that? Somebody out there respects my brain," Larry said to Crystal.

"Is this what you do for NASA?" she asked him sweetly.

"Pretty much," said Larry, helping the kids sort the tickets into piles of fives.

A RUBBER GECKO SQUEEZED tight in his chubby hand, David drifted off to sleep in the backseat of Larry's car. A second glance in the rearview mirror told Larry that Jennifer wasn't far behind. Her eyes had a dreamy look, and her blinks were long and slow.

He leaned toward Crystal and whispered. "Did we keep them out too late?" It had been a long time since his son Steve had been this age, and Larry couldn't remember bed times.

Not that he'd ever paid that much attention to the details of childrearing. If he started work in his study at six, he often didn't notice the time until well after midnight. Elizabeth was the reason Steve had survived childhood.

"They just had a good time," said Crystal. "I won't have any trouble getting them up for school."

"They're staying overnight with you?"

She nodded, a flinch of distress crossing her face. "I'm not sure what time Amber will get home."

Larry nodded his understanding.

None of his business, of course. But what kind of a

mother partied on a weeknight, potentially compromising her children's education?

"What about you?" asked Crystal. "You have school tomorrow."

"Classes are done," said Larry. "I'll mostly be compiling research over the summer."

"Really? What are you researching?"

Larry hated this part. No matter how hard he tried to keep it simple, people's eyes inevitably glazed over when he talked about his work. At parties, most people found a quick excuse to walk away.

"It's not all that interesting."

"Don't mollycoddle me. I handled your IQ, didn't I?"

"Fine," said Larry. "I'm researching physical and hydrodynamical modeling for galactic superwinds."

She blinked.

He took a breath, might as well find out now if she was going to walk away. "Specifically," he continued, "the physical origin of X-ray emissions created when supernova remnants overlap in the star-forming regions of space. They form highly pressurized bubbles that burst into intergalactic space, redistributing mass and heat."

The engine and tire noise filled in the silence.

"So, you don't know yet what makes the X-ray emissions," she said.

It was Larry's turn to blink. "You got that?"

"Well, it may be rocket science, buddy. But it wasn't like there were any new words in those sentences."

He stared at her as long as he dared without crashing the car. "You understood what I just said?"

"Don't get too impressed. It's not like you can take me into the lab to help with the hydrodynamical modeling."

Larry was speechless.

She took in his expression, an edge coming into her voice. "You never did ask me my IQ."

"Well…I…" To be honest, Larry hadn't been looking for intelligence from Crystal.

No. Wait. That sounded awful. She was obviously smart. Her sense of humor was sharp and sophisticated.

She glanced back at Jennifer.

Larry followed her gaze in the mirror and discovered the young girl was asleep along with her brother.

"You were too busy focusing on my hair," hissed Crystal. "And my…other assets."

"Whoa," Larry put in. "I've never once fixated on your physical attributes over your personality." He paused. "Okay, maybe the million-dollar ass comment was out of line. But it happens to be true." Whatever else she had, Crystal was the most beautiful woman he'd ever met.

"Ask me my IQ," she repeated.

The defiance in her voice gave him pause. "What's your IQ?"

"One fifty-two."

Okay. He was officially impressed. That number put her in the top one percent of his students. "Why didn't you say something?"

"Until now, I didn't think it mattered."

"It doesn't." He knew she was smart. He simply hadn't known how smart.

"Should we compare bank balances next?" she asked. "See who can pee the farthest?"

"You're a girl."

"And you're a metaphor-phobe."

"I don't think that's a real word."

"Hey, who around here has a graduate degree in English?"

"You do," he admitted.

They were both silent, while Larry made the last turn before the Softco Machine Works building.

"Are you really upset?" he asked.

"Not that much," she admitted.

"I like that you understand what I'm doing. I didn't mean to sound so surprised."

"And I didn't mean to go all ballistic feminist on you. I'm glad you like my…brain. Few people hang around long enough to see it."

"Their loss," Larry said softly, reaching for her hand.

Her fingers curled around his, and something felt totally right about the touch.

She closed her eyes and tipped her head back against the headrest. "What are we doing here, Larry?"

"I haven't a clue," he admitted. "You want to stop?"

To his relief, she shook her head.

He pulled into the parking lot of Softco, driving around the building to the back staircase that led to her apartment.

He killed the engine and flipped the catch on his seat belt. Jennifer's eyes blinked blearily open, but David stayed sound asleep.

"I'll carry him up," Larry whispered into the silence.

Crystal smiled her appreciation, and she opened her door, flipping the seat forward to help Jennifer out.

Larry bundled David into his arms, making sure the gecko didn't get dropped. Then he followed Crystal and Jennifer up the long staircase.

The dog named Rufus was waiting for them in the compact kitchen.

"Oh, man," Crystal moaned. "The poor guy needs a walk."

"I'll take him," Larry immediately offered, since, obviously, Crystal couldn't leave the children to walk the dog.

After settling David in the spare bedroom, Larry

clipped the leash on Rufus. The dog seemed more than willing to come with him, and Larry followed Crystal's directions to a pathway that was partially lighted by the overhead lights of the parking lot.

It was a quick walk, and soon they were trotting back up the staircase.

Larry knocked gently on the door, and Crystal opened it, still in her pale-blue dress, but now with bare feet.

"Thanks," she breathed, stepping out of the way. "I know you don't like me to call you nice."

He moved inside. "Couldn't you call me rugged or macho or something instead?"

"It was very macho of you to walk my dog."

"That's better," he acknowledged, pulling the door closed behind him and removing Rufus's leash.

"Coffee?" asked Crystal.

He glanced at his watch. "You sure it's not too late?"

"Nine-thirty?"

"You do have to get up for school in the morning."

Crystal crossed to the cupboards, opened the corner one, then stretched up to reach the bright red mugs on the top shelf. The action pulled up her hem, revealing a few more inches of shapely thigh.

Larry felt a pulse throb through his brain.

"Cream or sugar?" she asked.

"Black," he responded, dragging his gaze away.

She set the cups on the countertop, and her dress settled back into place.

The coffeemaker finished filling the carafe, and she poured two steaming cups, taking hers black as well. Then she handed one to Larry, nodding to the small, connected living-room area.

Rufus followed at Larry's heels.

Crystal took one end of the burgundy couch, and Larry sat down in the other, setting his mug on the end table beside him. The dog curled up next to his feet.

"We okay?" he asked her.

She nodded, crooking one knee and planting her back against the arm of the sofa so that she faced him.

He nodded toward the bedroom. "They going to be okay?"

"I hope so," said Crystal. "Zane won't hang around long. I just hope…" She got a faraway look in her eyes.

"Hope what?" he prompted.

"Last time he did this, things got ugly for Amber."

A horrible thought came into Larry's mind. "Is he abusive?"

"Not physically. Certainly emotionally." Crystal paused for a sip of her coffee. "Let's just say my sister has a troubled relationship with alcohol. Normally, she's fine. But in times of stress, she leans on it a bit too much for support. And the last time Zane left, it was a time of stress. I ended up keeping Jennifer and David here for a month until she got herself straightened out. I have a feeling it's going to happen again."

Rufus gave a little moan, shifting onto his side and stretching his legs out on the wooden floor.

"How long ago was that?" Larry asked.

"Two years."

"So, the kids remember?"

She gave a nod. "They remember."

Larry's gaze flicked to the door of the spare bedroom. "What about you?" he asked Crystal.

She looked puzzled. "Do *I* remember?"

"Any exes in your past likely to rear their heads?"

"My husband died two years ago."

Larry felt an instant pang of empathy. "I'm so sorry. I lost my wife, Libby, three years ago."

"Did you love her?" asked Crystal.

"Very much."

"I didn't love Simon." Crystal surprised him by saying. Then she gave a nervous laugh. "That sounds callous, doesn't it? But it's true."

"You married a man you didn't love?"

That definitely puzzled Larry. Crystal must have had her pick of a thousand men.

"I thought I loved him. Doesn't that sound pathetic? I saw what I wanted to see, until I couldn't lie to myself anymore."

"What was it you didn't see?"

"His fixation on my body."

"Ouch," said Larry, feeling even guiltier than he had before. That must be why she'd jumped down his throat.

"To the exclusion of anything else," she elaborated. "Simon and I had other problems." She lifted her coffee mug in a mock toast. "He loved the red dress."

"You don't have to wear the red dress," Larry quickly put in.

"I know," she said. "Trust me when I tell you, I'm never wearing anything I don't want to wear, ever again."

Yet, she'd offered to wear the red dress for him. Larry didn't want to speculate about what that meant. Well, he did want to speculate, but he knew that was dangerous territory.

"I'd asked him for a divorce," she said, eyes getting a faraway look. "The night before he was killed. I was all set to divorce him, then suddenly I was the grieving widow."

Larry couldn't even fathom her experience. He'd mourned Libby for months, years even, taking solace in his work. "How was Simon killed?"

"Scuba equipment failure. He was in the Navy. What about Libby?"

"Heart attack," said Larry, even now struggling to keep the emotion out of his voice. "We didn't even know there was a problem with her heart."

Crystal watched his expression closely.

"It was people like you that made me feel like a fake," she whispered. "People who deserved the sympathy, the cards, the flowers and the eulogy. Through it all, I wanted to stand up and shout that I was a fraud. I was going to *divorce* the man. But I knew it wouldn't have helped. Other people needed to grieve, and they needed me to play my role. So I pretended I'd loved him, pretended I cried and pretended he was the paragon they made him out to be at the memorial service."

"You did the right thing," Larry offered.

She wrapped her arms around herself in a hug. "And then there's his service pension and life insurance." Her voice went lower still. "I can't spend it. Every penny of that money is still sitting in the bank."

Larry glanced around the plainly furnished apartment. "You are his widow. You're legally entitled—"

She shook her head emphatically.

"You have to do something with the money."

"Maybe if I have kids someday. Maybe for Jennifer's and David's educations. But not for me."

"Penance?" asked Larry.

"Integrity," she responded.

He drained his coffee cup. "I can respect that."

The woman had brains and integrity. He admired both. She looked so vulnerable curled up under the soft lamplight.

The urge to draw her into his arms was definitely growing strong. He forced himself to stand up, determined to get out of here before he did something both stupid and inappropriate.

CHAPTER FOUR

CRYSTAL WAS DREAMING OF expressive, hazel eyes, broad shoulders and tousled, dark hair. Larry drew her into his arms, whispering in her ear. She couldn't make out the words, but she could feel the puff of his breath on her skin.

He was panting.

Then his cold, wet nose touched her shoulder.

Wait a minute.

She blinked her eyes in the dim light, coming face-to-face with Rufus.

Crystal groaned.

The dog cocked his head, ascertained she was awake, then turned toward the door. Two paces later, he stopped and looked back, obviously expecting her to follow.

"Now?" she asked aloud.

His brows knit apologetically.

She supposed this was what she got for taking in a geriatric dog.

She threw back the covers, planting her bare feet on the woven mat, then tugging her light, sleeveless nightgown down her thighs.

"All right," she told the dog, following behind. "I'll open the door, but you're on your own out there."

Hopefully, Rufus would be smart enough to water a tree behind the back fence and hightail it back into the apartment. She took her responsibility as a pet owner seriously. But she took her responsibility as a babysitting auntie more seriously.

She followed Rufus through the living room where, to her surprise, he veered off to the spare bedroom.

"Hey," she hissed. "No. This way."

Again, he stopped, glancing over his shoulder, waiting patiently.

Then she heard it.

Muffled sobs coming from the kids' room.

She quickly scooted past Rufus to find David, his face burrowed in his pillow, his little body quivering beneath the sheet.

"Hey, buddy," she crooned, smoothing his dark hair and crouching down beside the bed.

She gave Rufus a grateful scratch on the head.

"What's wrong?" she asked gently, trying not to wake Jennifer who was in the other twin bed across the room.

David shook his head, sniffing and drawing in a shuddering breath.

She grabbed a tissue from the bedside table and handed it to him.

He haphazardly wiped his nose.

"Are you sad?" asked Crystal.

He shook his head.

"Scared?"

A small, hesitant nod.

"Did you have a bad dream?"

He nodded again.

"Come here," Crystal groaned, slipped her arms around his waist. "Give me a hug."

He came willingly out of the bed in his Superman pajamas, and she slid down to the floor, sitting him across her lap. His skinny arms went around her neck, and he tucked his face against her shoulder.

"Can you tell me about it?" she asked.

"It was…" He took three rapid indrawn breaths. "A *monster*."

"Oh, sweetheart." She rubbed his back. "No wonder you were scared."

His arms tightened.

"But it's all over," she crooned.

"He was big and hairy, and he roared like an angry lion."

"Auntie Crystal's here now." She tried again.

"And I tried to run. But my legs were stuck, and then…and then…"

Crystal's heart went out to him.

"Mommy came," David whimpered.

"Did Mommy save you?" asked Crystal.

David shook his head. "The monster got Mommy."

Crystal's heart lodged in her throat.

The monster was big and hairy, and he yelled.

She nearly groaned out loud. There was every possibility the monster was Zane.

She brushed David's sweaty hair from his face. "You know the monster's not real, don't you?"

He hesitated, but then he nodded.

"Dreams are just your brain making up crazy pictures."

David nodded again.

Crystal drew him away so she could see his face in the dim light.

"I once dreamed I landed on the moon," she told him. "And I met a pink bunny. She was made entirely of cotton candy, except she had licorice whiskers." Crystal wrinkled her nose then made a show of licking her lips. "She looked delicious."

David cracked a smile.

"So I asked her." Crystal paused. "Can you guess what I asked her?"

David shrugged.

"I asked if I could eat her tail."

His eyes went wide, while Crystal made up the sweetest, tamest dream story she could conjure.

"She told me yes," said Crystal. "She said it wouldn't hurt, and her tail would grow back."

"Did you eat it?" asked David.

"You bet," said Crystal. "And then her friend Bobo came along. Can you guess what Bobo was made of?"

David pursed his little lips. "Marshmallows?"

"Yes," said Crystal. "Bobo was a little wiener dog made out of marshmallows."

"Shouldn't he be made of wieners?"

"Like I said, dreams are crazy." She rolled her eyes. "A wiener dog made out of marshmallows. Isn't that the silliest thing?"

"The silliest thing would be the Mallo-Puffs Man made out of wieners."

Crystal giggled. "That would be sillier," she agreed. She rubbed a finger across the tip of his nose. "But not as tasty."

"Did you eat the marshmallow dog?"

"Only his tail. That's the way it was on the moon. You could eat the tails, but nothing else."

David sobered. "I wish I had candy dreams."

"What's your favorite candy?"

"Caramel."

"And what's your favorite animal?"

He thought for a moment. "An elephant."

"And what would a caramel elephant be named?"

"Mr. Sticky."

"Great name."

David nodded.

"When you lie down again—"

His arms convulsively tightened around her neck.

"—I want you to think about all the adventures Mr. Sticky could have." She almost said on the moon, but quickly switched the thought. "In Candy Land," she finished.

"What if the monster comes back?"

"In Candy Land," Crystal said softly, "monsters are made of ice cream. And since Candy Land is warm, they melt away."

David looked skeptical.

"Tell you what," she said, trying one last idea. "How would you feel if I let Rufus sleep up on the bed with you?"

David looked at Rufus then back at Crystal. "Really?"

She nodded. "Really."

David compressed his lips bravely. "Okay."

Crystal smiled. "Good. Hop up then."

He straightened his skinny legs, standing to climb back under the covers.

She tucked him in, then patted the foot of the bed. "Come on, Rufus."

The dog looked at her as if she'd lost her mind.

"Up here," she said encouragingly with another pat.

Rufus cocked his head, eyes narrowing.

"Come on, Rufus," called David.

The dog gave Crystal one last, searching, suspicious look. Then he rose to his feet, gathered his body and jumped onto the bed.

"Good, boy," she sang, scratching behind both his ears. "Now, lie down."

She'd already learned that lie down was a familiar

command to Rufus. He curled his body next to David's feet, then dropped his head down on his front paws.

She moved back to the head of the bed. "You going to be okay?" she asked David.

He nodded.

"Remember, Mr. Sticky and his adventures in Candy Land."

"With his faithful dog, Rufus?"

"What's Rufus made of?"

"Bubble gum."

"Perfect," said Crystal, giving David a final kiss on the forehead.

"G'night, Auntie Crystal."

"Good night, David."

She glanced over to Jennifer's bed.

The girl's eyes were open.

Crystal moved across the room and straightened the covers. "Good night to you, too, sweetheart."

"I like Rufus," Jennifer whispered.

"I like Rufus, too," said Crystal as Jennifer's eyes fluttered close.

Crystal walked to the bedroom door, pausing to gaze back at her beautiful niece and nephew and the somewhat scruffy Lab who seemed to be standing guard over them.

Her tomorrow would revolve around another dinner with Larry. But she'd have to find a way to talk to Amber, as well. If Zane was the monster in David's nightmare, then he had to get out of their lives—permanently, and soon.

AFTER LIBBY DIED, LARRY'S family and friends had told him to get on with his life. Get a hobby, they'd said, don't work so hard. As if throwing himself into his work wasn't the best and only way to keep from going insane with grief.

He'd ignored them, and his approach had worked. For a while.

But on this last wedding anniversary, something inside him snapped. He realized he needed to rejoin the human race. And to do that, he needed to take on something brand new, something totally unconnected with Libby. So, he'd taken his family's advice, used some of the money he'd earned through mathematically calculating the stock market, and bought himself a hobby—a big, old Victorian house on the shores of Myrtle Pond.

Two hours northeast of Charlotte, the tiny community of Myrtle Pond was on the edge of the national forest. The road in was worn and potholed. He had a total of fifteen neighbors. Calling the big house a fixer-upper was being kind, but it was exactly what he wanted, needed.

He'd stocked up on power tools and two-by-fours and transported them to the house last month. Today, since he'd been up at four o'clock—which wasn't a problem, because he'd been cursed his entire life with a need for only four hours sleep—he'd fired up his compact Cessna airplane and flown from Charlotte to Myrtle Pond.

By one in the afternoon, crowbar in hand, he was staring at a pile of broken drywall, bent nails and the bare two-by-four frame of the formal dining room.

"Do you have the first clue about what you're doing?" came a man's voice from behind him.

Larry turned to see his nearest neighbor Nash Walkins standing in work boots, blue jeans and a faded T-shirt. Nash wore his usual orange baseball cap, and his burly arms were folded across his chest.

He owned a fishing store and boat rental business now, but Larry had learned he was once an architect in New York City.

"Not even the slightest," Larry admitted. He'd hoped that by revealing the guts of the sagging wall, it would become obvious how to fix it. He had a number of reference books and some faded building plans for a similar house.

He'd decided to start with the dining room, since it seemed to be in the worst shape, followed by the upstairs bathroom, the kitchen and, well, pretty much everything else except the master bedroom, which had been redecorated by the previous owner.

Nash took a step forward. "You're gonna want a jack to support that while you cut out the dry rot."

A jack. Good idea. "Can I get one around here?"

"You'll have to head up to Asheboro. Drucker's will have them in stock."

Larry nodded. Not today, then. "I have to get back to Charlotte by six."

"Giving a lecture?"

Larry hesitated for only a moment. "I've got a date." He liked the sound of that. He really liked the sound of that.

Nash grinned his admiration. "I don't suppose she has a sister."

"Her sister's reconciling with her ex."

"Now, that's a damn shame."

"Are you going through a dry spell?" Larry had been up to Myrtle Pond at least once a week for the past two months. From what he could see, there was a fairly steady parade of attractive women on Nash's deck next door.

"Always on the lookout."

"For the right woman or the next woman?"

Nash measured the height of the dining room wall. "For the next right woman, of course."

"Then it's not going to be Crystal's sister," Larry warned. "Or anyone else she knows, for that matter."

Nash selected a couple of two-by-fours from the pile at one end of the room. "Don't worry. I won't mess things up with your girlfriend."

"Not girlfriend," Larry corrected.

Nash turned a dial on the table saw. "First date?"

"Second. Well, second if you count Pizza Heaven."

Nash paused and looked back at Larry. "You took a woman to Pizza Heaven? How long did you say you were married?"

"Thirty years."

"Man, are you out of practice."

"Her niece and nephew came along," Larry defended.

"You got any metal strapping?"

"Sure." Larry exited to the living room, hunting his way through a line of cardboard boxes.

He'd pretty much given the guy at the hardware store free rein to load him up with tools and supplies. He'd also ordered a series of home renovation books. He was becoming familiar with the terminology and tool usage, but he was stifling the urge to read his way through the series before he got started. The whole point of this hobby was to get his nose out of books and to move his mind from the theoretical to the practical.

The table saw was whining when he reentered the dining room.

"You might want to think about steel-toed boots," said Nash, glancing pointedly at Larry's tan suede sneakers.

"Guess I haven't made it to that chapter yet."

Nash gave a barrel laugh. "Grab a set of cutters. We're going to strap three two-by-fours together and brace the frame." He pointed. "Then you can start cutting out the dry rot."

"Got it," said Larry, happy to have the advice.

"Don't you want to know how long?" asked Nash.

"How long what?"

"How long to make the straps?"

Larry gave Nash a look of disbelief. "It's three two-by-fours. Are you seriously asking if I'll have trouble with the math?"

"My mistake," said Nash.

"Don't worry about it," said Larry. "I'm still getting over the fact that Fibonacci seemed to have no role in the development of standard building materials."

"Maybe not. But the golden ratio is everywhere in architecture."

"Not in this house," said Larry. Damn shame, that. From the Parthenon to Notre Dame to the United Nations Building, the ratio of 1.618 had been used to provide beauty and balance.

Then, Larry had an idea. A fabulous, exciting idea. "At least, not yet," he added.

Nash glanced around. "We're going to rebuild your house using Fibonacci numbers?"

"Why not?" The more Larry thought about it, the more he liked it. It would help him engage in the project in a more meaningful way. He could work on the plans while he was back in Charlotte, making his time at Myrtle Pond more efficient.

"Sounds like fun," said Nash. "But first, can we make sure the wall doesn't fall down?"

TALKING WITH NASH TODAY about the golden ratio had Larry analyzing Crystal's face across the candlelit table at Rouladen's. He could easily see why she had been picked as a model. Beauty and balance. Her lips, her nose, her chin her forehead. He was willing to bet she was a collection of one-point-six-one-eights.

He smiled.

"What?" she asked, pausing, her wineglass poised in midair.

"I was thinking you have phi all over your face."

Her eyes narrowed.

"Math humor," he confessed.

"You think my face is funny?"

"I think your face is perfect. Mathematically speaking. The ratio of your nose to your lips, and your eyes to your chin, your pupils to your eyelashes, and the spiral of your ears."

"My ears?"

"Yes." He let his gaze rest on her perfect ears.

"This is a good thing?"

"It's a very good thing. It means that not only me, but everybody in the world thinks you're beautiful."

She set down the glass of merlot, lips thinning, and a line forming between her eyebrows. "Is that what you're looking for?"

It was his turn to squint in confusion.

"A mathematically perfect woman?" she asked.

"I'm not looking for anything," he answered honestly. And he wasn't. Crystal had breezed into his life that morning in the garage, and their connection was something he wanted to explore. But, beyond that, he had no expectations whatsoever.

"Maybe to give you mathematically perfect children?" she continued.

"Huh?" Larry had already raised his son. Grandchildren might be nice at some point, but they'd have nothing to do with mathematics—except that one and one sometimes made three.

"They talked about the golden ratio and perfect beauty, while I was modeling."

"And you have it." It was a simple fact.

"I don't want it," she responded sharply.

"If it helps, balanced facial features also tend to denote good health."

"Lucky me."

"Is there some reason you don't want to be beautiful?" It hardly struck him as a severe handicap.

She gave a frustrated sigh. "It gets in the way."

"Of what?"

"Of people, men in particular, having any interest in anything else."

"We can talk about your IQ for a while. Or your cookbook. Or your niece and nephew. Or your dog. How is Rufus, anyway?"

She didn't smile.

"Seriously," said Larry. "How is he?"

She finally seemed to relax. "I think he's still waiting for his owner to show up. But he was great last night. He woke me up when David was having a nightmare."

Larry was assailed by memories of Steven as a little boy. His bad dreams were few and far between. But every once in a while, he'd show up in their bedroom, his scruffy, brown teddy bear dangling from one hand.

"Is David okay now?" Larry asked.

"He seemed fine this morning. But I'm a little worried…."

Larry waited, while Crystal focused on the tiny, yellow flame flickering between them. The soft sounds of a string quartet and muted conversation floated around the high-ceilinged room.

"I'm afraid the monster in his dreams might be Zane."

Larry drew back. "Do you think Zane might harm the kids?"

"I asked Jennifer this morning, in an oblique sort of way. She said Zane yells a lot, but he doesn't throw things and he's never hurt David."

"Do you believe her?"

Crystal nodded. "But he's a loose cannon. He's all sweetness and light when he wants something. But once he wrings Amber dry, he can get mean."

"Did you talk to your sister about it?" Larry asked softly.

"She's on the manic high of Zane being back in her life."

"Anything I can do?"

Crystal shook her head. "I wish there was."

Larry felt a strong urge to take the worry out of her eyes, even if it was only temporarily. "In that case," he said, pulling his chair back and coming to his feet. "Would you like to dance?" He nodded to where a few other couples were swaying to the string quartet.

Crystal had worn her red dress, and she looked stunning. Even if she was shy of her beauty, Larry admitted he'd like nothing better than to hold her in his arms and be the envy of every man in the room.

She nodded and set her linen napkin on the table.

Larry moved forward to pull out her upholstered chair, watching with appreciation as she came to her feet.

"This music's slower than I'm used to," she told him, as he took her hand in his, leading her in a snaking pattern past a few occupied tables.

"Life's an adventure," he pointed out, taking her into his arms. She fit absolutely perfectly.

And she was a wonderful dancer, light on her feet, responsive, graceful. He caught the eyes of one gentleman watching from the sidelines, then another and another.

He couldn't help but smile to himself and pull her that little bit closer, molding her curves to his body.

"You're a great dancer," she whispered.

"So are you."

"I mean, really good," she insisted. "I'm just following along."

"Music is all math," he told her. "It's patterns and fractions, sound waves and Hertz frequencies. Ever wonder why C and G are consonant, while C and F sharp are discordant?"

"No," she answered.

"Really?"

"Do you ever just listen?"

"To what?"

He felt more than heard her soft chuckle.

"Do you ever simply think a piece of music sounds nice, or a flower is pretty?"

"Would you like to know why flowers are pleasing to our eyes?"

"No," she said again.

He drew back to look into her face. "You're not curious?"

"The world is not simply a living, breathing mathematical equation."

"Actually, it is."

"Larry," she warned.

"Your dress is beautiful," he told her.

A grin grew on her face. "Full stop?"

He matched her teasing smile. "I could tell you mathematically why, but I won't."

They gazed at each other for a few moments, still swaying to the soft music. He felt his heart beat deepen, and prickles of desire pop out on his skin.

"Tell me why you want to kiss me," she teased.

"There's a theorem involving pheromones and evolutionary computing, first postulated by Smythe and Heinz in the 1990s. But it gets complicated."

"You mean this can't be explained by simple mathematics?"

"Simple?" he scoffed. "I'm sure if we brought in enough variables, I could eventually come up with an algorithm for our specific—"

"Shut up and kiss me."

That was exactly what he should do. He should stop doing calculations, forget about the age difference, forget about everything but the magic he was feeling.

Larry stroked his palm over her impossibly soft cheek. He gazed into her jade green eyes, then stroked the pad of his thumb over her red lips.

He wanted this, wanted it so bad. But he forced himself to go slow, forced himself to keep it appropriate to the dance floor. Which proved more difficult than he'd imagined.

Her lips were sweet and soft, moist and tender. They parted ever so slightly, and his arm instantly tightened around her waist. She tipped her head, and he followed suit, fitting their mouths more firmly together.

His blood sang; the world blurred. It had been so long—*so* long since he'd held a woman in his arms, inhaled sweet perfume, tasted satin skin, felt soft curves pressed against his hard body.

The violin hit a high C, jolting him back to reality.

He forced himself to break the kiss, drawing back to the puff of her sigh.

"Sorry," he whispered, taking up the dance again.

"I'm not," she breathed back, falling into step.

Neither was he.

He wasn't sorry he kissed her. He was only sorry he'd had to stop. And he was already wondering when he'd get a chance to do it again.

CHAPTER FIVE

THE MEMORY OF THEIR KISS fresh in her mind, Crystal skipped up her apartment stairs in front of Larry. Rufus would be anxious to get out. But it could be a short walk. And then, as long as Larry was willing, and if there wasn't any mathematical law against it, they could try that kiss all over again. This time, there wouldn't be an audience, and there'd be no reason to cut it short.

"Crystal?"

She cringed at the sound of her mother's voice, followed by the slamming of a car door at the far side of the parking lot. She stopped midway up the staircase, turning around.

"Hi, Mom. You working late?" It wasn't unusual for her parents to be at the shop any hour of the day or night.

Larry followed Crystal's lead, walking back down the stairs as Stella crossed the parking lot under the bright overhead lights.

"Have you been out?" asked Stella, a critical eye going to Larry where the nearest light pooled around him.

"Mom, this is Larry Grosso," Crystal explained. "Dean Grosso's brother. We met at the track this weekend."

Stella's expression and demeanor instantly changed.

"Larry, this is my mother, Stella Hayes."

Stella eagerly held out her hand. "I believe we may have

met a few years back. I know your brother, of course. And Kent is your nephew, then?"

Larry smiled and shook her hand. "He is."

Stella glanced back and forth between the two. "Is there something I can help you with? Does one of the teams have a problem?"

Larry glanced to Crystal, obviously leaving the choice of an explanation to her. After a lightning fast debate inside her head, she decided to downplay the evening.

"Larry and I stopped for dinner," she told her mother, trying to make it sound casual, thankful she had a light, neutral wrap covering her red dress. "He's a mathematician." Okay, where to go from there? "We were talking about my cookbook." Not a complete lie, since the topic *had* come up at one point.

Stella's eyes narrowed. "There's math in your cookbook?"

"Anthropology," said Crystal, her mind beginning to scramble.

Thankfully, Larry picked up the ball. "There's a growing interest in abstract algebra," he said. "In conjunction with probability and statistics, of course. And particularly with an emphasis on derivation of pattern in the study of interinformant reliability, general interaction theory and systemic cultural continuity."

Stella blinked. "It's a cookbook."

"It's much more than just a cookbook," said Larry.

"There's math in everything," Crystal offered, and she could almost feel Larry's triumphant grin next to her.

Then Rufus, obviously hearing their voices, barked to be let out.

The shock was obvious on Stella's face. "Why do I hear a dog?" she demanded.

Crystal was momentarily speechless. She'd planned to

tell her parents about Rufus, of course. Well, only if she didn't hear from the police or the old man's relatives soon. But she was hoping to find the right moment. She didn't relish the idea of a lecture on the impracticality of pets when a person had a career to think about and didn't even have a permanent address.

"His name's Rufus," said Larry. "I'm doing some home renovations, and Crystal offered to keep him for a little while."

Crystal sent Larry a fleeting look of gratitude.

"Oh." Stella's expression mellowed.

Clearly, a Grosso dog was an entirely different matter.

"I should be heading home," said Stella. "It was nice to meet you, Larry."

"A pleasure," said Larry.

"I'll see you tomorrow, Mom," Crystal put in. She'd been busy with Jennifer and David today, but she'd be back in the office tomorrow to help out with whatever needed doing.

While her mother crossed to her car, Crystal and Larry headed back up the stairs.

"You do know I'm too old to be lying to someone's parents," said Larry as soon as the door closed behind them.

The purr of Stella's engine disappeared as she exited through the gate.

"Sorry," said Crystal with sincerity. "I didn't know what to say to her."

Larry nodded. "I had the same problem. 'I'm weighing the probability of kissing your daughter again' didn't seem quite right."

"Is that what you're doing?" asked Crystal, forgetting about her mother and focusing on Larry all over again.

"Of course, that's what I'm doing."

"What are the odds?"

"I'd give it a fifty-fifty," he said.

Crystal moved a little closer. "Better rework that equation, Professor."

"Yeah?"

"Yeah," she told him huskily. "I'm no rocket scientist, but I'd give it a ninety-five."

"For or against?"

"For."

"I like the way you do math."

"Do I get an A?"

"I don't know," he drawled. "Your theoretical work is top-notch, but this is *applied* mathematics."

Crystal blinked flirtatiously. "Then I guess I'd better get started on a real-world application."

His expression sobered. He took a step forward, then tipped her chin with his index finger. "Good. Because there's a particular theory I'd like to test."

His touch sent a cascade of desire coursing through her. She instantly remembered the taste of his lips, the strength of his embrace and the scent of his skin.

"Test away," she whispered.

He leaned forward.

Her eyes closed.

Rufus barked.

They turned in unison to stare at the dog who was all but twitching with the need to get out.

Larry sighed. "I'll take him."

"I'm sorry."

Larry reached for the leash. "You stay right there. Don't move."

"Yes, sir," she promised.

The door clicked shut, and Crystal stood in her dim kitchen picturing Larry and Rufus on the stairs, in the parking lot, out on the pathway.

She glanced at her watch, estimating five or so minutes for the walk if Rufus cooperated. Then her gaze caught his food dish, and she wondered if she should fill it. They didn't need an interruption from a hungry dog on top of everything else.

But she'd promised Larry she'd stay still. So she decided to leave the dish as it was.

But then her phone rang.

She checked her impulse to answer it and stayed where she was. Whoever it was could call back in the morning. It was probably her mother with more questions about Larry. Crystal sure didn't need that at the moment. It might even be a marketing firm. Who wanted to interrupt their evening for a marketing firm?

She squinted, trying to see the glowing number in the readout.

Amber.

Damn it. It could be important. She crossed the kitchen to the phone.

"Amber? Is everything okay?"

"It's fine. Why wouldn't it be? Where have you been?"

"I was out." Crystal paused. "Working with someone on my cookbook."

"I called earlier."

"But nothing's wrong?" Crystal reconfirmed, taking a seat on the sofa.

"I needed you to babysit."

"Again?"

The door opened, and Larry appeared with Rufus. Crystal glanced guiltily up at them.

Larry shook his head in resignation and hung Rufus's leash up on one of the coat hooks near the door.

"Zane's leaving tomorrow," said Amber.

Crystal felt a surge of hope. "Back to Atlanta?"

"He does have a job there."

"Really?"

"Don't sound so surprised. I told you he's changed."

Crystal didn't respond.

Amber gave a long-suffering sigh that transmitted her pitiful circumstances over the phone lines. "I'm going to miss him so much."

"You haven't seen him in months," Crystal felt compelled to point out.

Rufus sniffed at his empty dish, and Larry pointed to a cupboard, eyebrows raised in a question.

"What does that have to do with anything?" asked Amber, annoyance coming into her tone.

Crystal pointed to the dog food cupboard. "I just meant… Never mind." Her sister definitely wasn't in a mood to listen to reason.

"So, can you do it?" asked Amber.

"Do what?"

"Babysit tonight so I can say goodbye."

Crystal glanced at her watch. It was nearly ten o'clock. "This late?"

"There's a new club down on Elm Street."

"Who's paying?"

"What kind of a question is that?"

A stupid question. Amber was paying, of course.

Larry scooped some dry food into Rufus's dish and refilled the water bowl.

Crystal mouthed *thank you*.

"Aren't the kids asleep?" she asked Amber.

"Of course they're asleep."

"So, you want me to come over there." Crystal gave Larry a pained, apologetic look as he crossed the room to sit beside her.

"Could you?" asked Amber.

"Not really," Crystal responded. She'd do anything for her niece and nephew, but Amber needed to take some responsibility here.

Larry's strong arm went around her shoulders. He kissed the top of her head. "Do the kids need you?" he murmured.

Crystal glanced up at him. Yes, the kids needed her. There was no telling what Amber might do, no telling what Zane might pressure her into. She wished with all her heart that Amber was logical and trustworthy. But the truth was, Crystal couldn't begin to guess what Amber would do if she turned her down.

"Tell her yes," whispered Larry.

Crystal closed her eyes in disappointment, while Larry gave her a reassuring squeeze.

"What time will you be back home?" she asked her sister.

"Midnight," said Amber. "Maybe one at the latest."

"Make it midnight," Crystal insisted, knowing she was wasting her breath.

"Sure. Of course," Amber sang. "When can you be here?"

Crystal gazed steadily into Larry's dark, hazel eyes. "It'll take me a bit to get out the door."

"Hurry," said Amber.

"Goodbye," said Crystal, hitting the off button.

"I take it she has a date with Zane," said Larry, his fingers absently twirling Crystal's hair.

"He's leaving tomorrow."

"Hopefully for good."

"I sure hope so." She gave a hard sigh and dropped her head back against Larry's arm.

"Do we have time for a kiss?" he asked.

"Yes!" She straightened and turned to pucker. "Do it now. Quick. Before anything else can get in the way."

His hand slipped behind her head, fingers twining in her hair. "I was hoping for slow, but if that's not going to happen—"

And then his lips were on hers, harder than earlier, firm, confident and demanding. With his free hand, he tugged her up close.

His mouth was a fiery combination of moisture, suction, movement and exquisite taste. Her arms snaked around his neck, while her body hummed with fiery sensation. One kiss turned to two, then three, then four.

Finally, Larry grasped her upper arms, and set her away. "You have to go," he gasped, while she struggled to catch her breath.

"Uh…" She tried, temporarily unable to form words.

"To Amber's," he reminded her.

Crystal nodded. "Right." She hadn't *exactly* forgotten. But neither of them moved.

He dipped his head forward again, then stopped short before kissing her, muttering a pithy curse under his breath. "Come to Dover," he said. "This weekend."

The invitation shocked Crystal speechless.

"Separate rooms," he rushed on. "No expectations. We can take in the race, maybe drive to the coast. Zane will be out of the way, so you won't have any babysitting duties."

Crystal hesitated. Great as it sounded, her current financial circumstance didn't allow for impulsive weekend getaways. It was embarrassing, but she owed it to him to be honest. She didn't want him to think she wasn't interested.

"I really can't afford—"

He frowned. "Not this again. You'd be my guest."

Oh, no. Not happening. She shook her head. Dinner was one thing, but she wasn't letting him pay for her hotel.

"I wish you'd stop insulting me by trying to pay," he said.

"I can't let you pay for my weekend."

"Give me one good reason why not?"

"We're not dating."

"We just had dinner and a kiss. What's not dating about that?"

"You know what I mean," she elaborated. "We're not...*dating*."

"So you're saying, if I pay for your hotel room, I should expect you to have sex with me?"

"Don't be ridiculous." She didn't put out simply because a man dropped a few bucks. If that was the case, she'd have had a dozen lovers by now.

"Because that's where you're logic's leading," said Larry.

"My logic is leading to me paying for my own hotel room," she argued.

His voice turned authoritative. "Well, you can't. Because you're not willing to use Simon's money. Which I admire, by the way. And, I'd rather you didn't in this instance anyway. But that only leaves us with me paying. Which is what I want to do anyway, and you're simply going to have to live with it."

"That's some very convoluted, circular logic you got going there, Professor."

"I'm desperate."

She struggled not to smile at his expression.

"Say yes," he pressed. "And I'll go back to my regular, linear self."

Crystal hesitated. A weekend in Dover. Separate rooms. Nothing but fun and relaxation for two whole days.

What was to stop her, really?

Wait a minute. There *was* something stopping her. "I can't leave Rufus." It's not like she could ask her mother to take care of him.

"Bring him along," said Larry

That offer surprised her. The kids were one thing. "You don't mind if I bring the dog?"

"Why not? I'll find an inn that allows pets. And he can stay at one of the Grosso motor homes at the track."

Crystal turned the idea over in her mind. "What about the plane?" Surely they weren't going to drive five hundred miles to Dover.

"We'll rent him a crate for the plane. It's only an hour."

"This is crazy," she felt compelled to interject.

His lips curved up in a slow grin. "Isn't it? It's not at all like me. Is it anything like you?"

"It's exactly like me," she admitted. That's why she was still living above her parents' business, with no money, a half-written cookbook anthology and a big, old stray dog.

He grasped her hand and kissed the back of her knuckles. "Then, let's do it."

There was something about his expression that called to her and something about his tone that was infectious.

She glanced to Rufus who had found his spot on the mat. "What do you say, boy? You up for a getaway weekend?"

Rufus blinked his dark-brown eyes up at them and gave a wide, toothy yawn.

"That was a yes," said Larry, with conviction.

Crystal couldn't help but laugh.

His grip tightened on her hands, and his expression turned serious. "Say yes."

She took a bracing breath. "Yes."

ON DELAWARE BAY, FORTY-FIVE minutes from the track at Dover, Larry pulled into the driveway of a two-story Cape Cod-style house.

"Hope you don't mind," he said, nodding toward the house. "I thought Rufus would like this better than a motel room." Larry killed the engine on the SUV they'd rented at the airport, and the air-conditioning switched off.

Crystal gazed in awe at the wide front porch, two stately, white-sided stories, and the profusion of begonias against an emerald-green lawn. Bright flower pots decorated a winding, stone walkway that led from the driveway to the front staircase. The ocean was visible beyond, between the widely spaced houses on the quiet street.

"Three bedrooms and four bathrooms," said Larry. "So, you'll have plenty of privacy."

"It's magnificent," Crystal breathed.

He grinned. "It belongs to a friend of Milo's, my grandfather. It fronts onto the beach. The kitchen is fully equipped. But, don't worry, I'm not expecting you to cook."

"I can cook," she offered. "At least that would be some kind of a contribution to the weekend."

He opened the driver's door, letting in the salt tang and the humid, ninety-degree heat. "Don't be ridiculous."

She followed suit, stepping onto the warm concrete driveway, while extracting her overnight bag from behind the seat. "I'll have you know I've tested every one of the recipes in my book," she told him. "Bring me a bucket of clams, baby, and I'll show you what chowder is."

He stared at her over the top of the vehicle. "That's not the point."

"What is the point?"

"Enjoying ourselves."

"I enjoy cooking."

"You'll enjoy Delveccio's more." Larry ambled toward the rear door to liberate Rufus. "Fine wine, local specialties, international flare. The man was trained in Paris."

"We can buy fine wine at the corner store."

"Not the 1992 Le Comte Bordeaux."

"Larry." She sighed in frustration.

He glanced up. "What?"

"Let me win one, okay?"

His eyebrows drew together in puzzlement.

"An argument," she elaborated.

"This is an argument?"

"Of course it's an argument."

He popped open the hatchback. "Wow. Your threshold for argument it pretty low."

Rufus scooted out from beside the airline crate and plopped to the ground.

"What would you call it?" she asked.

"A discussion," said Larry.

Fine. She wasn't going to start a whole new argument over semantics. "You think you could maybe let me win a discussion once in a while."

Larry grinned and slammed the door closed, while Rufus put his nose down to check out the lawn and the begonias. "Sure."

"So, we're eating in?"

"We can decide that later."

Her free hand rose to her hip. "How exactly does that mean I win?"

Larry gave a shrug. "Well, I didn't win." His tone turned authoritative. "And there are two of us in this discussion. Logic dictates, that if it's not X it must, therefore be Y."

"And I'm Y?"

"In this equation, yes, you are."

"Well, the answer didn't go in Y's favor."

"We don't know that yet."

"It could just as easily go to X."

Larry liberated her bag from her hand. "Now, *this* is an argument." But his voice was mild, his expression unconcerned, as he turned and headed for the front door.

Crystal took a hop step to keep up with his longer legs on the stone pathway.

"You don't have an answer for that, do you?" she challenged, even as she acknowledged her feeling of triumph was disproportional to the situation. "That's why you walked away."

He didn't answer.

"Face it, Professor," she continued. "I'm winning this *discussion,* and your ego's feeling the pain."

He inserted the key into the front door of the house. "You think this is about my ego?"

"I absolutely do."

He opened the door wide and gestured for her to precede him. "Ever consider that I simply want you to enjoy a nice Bordeaux?"

She marched inside. "Not even for a second."

Then her voice trailed away as her gaze caught on the plush furniture, the gleaming hardwood floors, fine oil paintings and massive windows overlooking a white sand beach and rolling azure waves.

She vaguely heard Larry set down the bags and close the door after Rufus followed them in. An air conditioner hummed gently in the background; otherwise the house was silent. It smelled of lemon polish and the fresh flower arrangements that sat on a rectangular table in the entryway and on the low coffee table nestled between two cream-colored couches in front of a stone fireplace.

"Wow," she breathed, moving on autopilot toward the dining room to open a set of French doors that led to a wide, cedar deck. Rattan chairs with plump taupe cushions were placed around small redwood tables, while one end of the deck was dominated by a glass-topped dining table and a massive, stainless-steel barbecue.

Crystal nodded to the barbecue. "Any chance we can grill steaks tonight?"

"Sure," said Larry from where he'd followed her outside.

She turned to contemplate his expression. "You gave in awfully easy on that."

He moved up behind her, wrapping his arms around her waist and pulling her against the cradle of his body. "That's because you really do want to barbecue. You're not just offering to be polite."

She nestled against him, trying to remember the last time she'd felt so secure in a man's arms. Maybe never. There was something about Larry's voice, his touch, his scent, that made her feel like she never wanted to leave his side.

He might not have any expectations of this weekend, but her expectations were growing by leaps and bounds. She couldn't imagine anything nicer than spending a warm, romantic evening overlooking the Atlantic, followed by a night in a big, comfortable bed with Larry.

The strength of her desire surprised her. Sure, his kiss had been off the charts. But it was a pretty big leap from a first proper kiss to a night in bed.

She felt his lips touch the top of her head, kissing her, softly, gently, lingering there while he inhaled the scent of her shampoo. It was an undeniably sexy move.

She stayed still and silent, not wanting to break the mood. White foam burbled its way on shore; a few gulls danced above the scattered sailboats and yachts in the bay. By the beach on the far side, compact boutique hotels rose against the blue sky, while dots that were people milled about on the faraway sand.

There were houses on either side of them, but hedges and tall maple trees protected their privacy. A couple with a little white dog walked barefoot along the beach below, leaving footprints that were quickly obliterated by the waves.

Larry's arms reflexively squeezed, and she covered his hands with her own. He leaned down and kissed her temple, then her cheek, then the shell of her ear. "You're beautiful," he whispered, holding her close.

How many times had she heard that? How many times had some man waxed poetic about her face or her legs.

And how many times had she considered he might be talking about something more than her physical attributes?

Never.

But with Larry, she instinctively believed he'd seen past the golden ratio, past the physical beauty she'd always found to be more of a curse than a blessing. When he called her beautiful, he didn't simply mean she'd impress his buddies, or turn the heads of strangers who watched them cross the dance floor, or that she'd look good in their photo Christmas card.

Her heart glowed warm with the compliment.

"Thank you," she said simply.

They silently breathed in the fresh air, his chest rising in sync with hers. A breeze gusted against them, blowing her loose hair, while a gull called in the sky, swooping on the air currents.

Crystal settled more comfortably against Larry's body. "What now?" she asked.

His pause was telling, and she hoped he was thinking the same thing as her. She screwed up her courage, getting ready to suggest they check out one of the bedrooms upstairs.

CHAPTER SIX

"WALK WITH ME?" LARRY ASKED in a gentle voice, even as he backed off and put an inch of space between them.

Crystal squelched her burgeoning fantasy. She was obviously getting away from herself on the romance front. They were staying in separate rooms, and he'd made it perfectly clear he was expecting a platonic weekend.

Maybe he wasn't ready to move past his wife? He'd certainly made it clear that he'd loved her.

"Sure," said Crystal.

He gave her a brisk rub on the upper arms before letting her go. Then he headed inside and retrieved the leash, calling to Rufus. He secured the sliding door and opened the low gate at the top of the staircase that led to the beach.

Crystal turned her attention to the strip of sculpted, white sand. An enthusiastic Rufus trotted down the narrow staircase in front of them.

The tide was high, and a few fluffy clouds made their way across the open blue sky. Crystal pulled off her sandals and dropped them on the bottom stair. She fluffed her hair and took a deep breath of the fresh air, while Rufus trundled, nose down, toward the pulsing foam.

"Should we keep him on the leash?" Larry asked as the dog investigated a bulb of yellow seaweed.

"I don't think he'll go far."

There was no one else in sight. The couple with the white dog were long gone. Rufus trotted ahead on the wet sand, in the general direction of the town site. He found another scent trail, followed it for a few yards, then took off on a new tangent.

Larry stretched out his hand, capturing Crystal's and twining their fingers together. She let herself sink into the silence of the sky and the gentle whoosh of the waves as they gradually relinquished their hold on the mushy sand.

"Ever been sailing?" Larry asked, his gaze going to the white flashes of sail far out in the bay and the bare masts rocking closer in at anchor.

"Recreational pursuits were never high on my parents' list of priorities."

"Yeah?"

She shook her head. "No picnics, no camping, no amusement parks."

"What did you do on vacation?"

She listed off on her fingers. "Marketing trips, tool trade shows…"

"I hear you. I spent my formative years in NASCAR garages or at midget tracks."

"Midget tracks?"

"That's where Dean got started." Larry smiled, but there was something other than joy in his eyes. "All racing, all the time."

"Did you race?"

"Nope. I spent a lot of time in the pits with my nose in a textbook."

Crystal paused, trying to picture Larry as a young boy, next to the toolboxes, fuel tanks and spare parts. "Was it hard?" she asked.

"I liked textbooks."

"No. I mean, was it hard having your family focus exclusively on Dean's dreams and not on yours?" At least Crystal had an ally in Amber. Amber had hated business trips, too.

"I didn't need a pit crew, and I didn't need to drive from town to town. I could do what I loved anywhere."

"You know what I mean."

Larry shrugged. "When you live in a NASCAR family, you live in a NASCAR family. And we love each other. We're an extremely close family."

Crystal felt her heart softening. "Still—"

"It was a long time ago," he said.

"It wasn't fair."

He stopped, turned to face her, and cocked his head to one side. "Hey."

"It wasn't fair," she repeated.

A grin grew on his face. "If life was fair, sweetheart, we'd be living in a whole different world."

The endearment spurred the butterflies in her stomach.

Then a wet Rufus bounded up, shaking his fur and dropping a piece of driftwood at Larry's feet.

Larry gamely reached down and tossed the stick into the waves. "See that? Rufus's got his priorities straight."

"Did you even feel pressured?" she asked as Rufus plunged into the surf.

"About what?"

"To go into racing."

"You bet. Milo is practically a force of nature, and Juliana only wanted Milo to be happy. Together, they wanted me to race. It was hard to stick to my guns." His expression turned thoughtful. "So, I was always careful to put as many choices as I could in front of Steve. And he decided he liked racing. Go figure."

"I was a disappointment to my parents," Crystal admitted.

"They wanted a boy to carry on the family business?"

She shook her head. "There are plenty of female machinists in the world. And they'd have settled for an accountant or a marketing manager."

"But they got a creative writer."

Crystal flicked her windblown hair away from her face, while Rufus made a neat turn in the waves, the stick clasped in his mouth. "Who moonlights delivering car parts."

"What about Amber?"

"Amber got married and gave them grandchildren."

"Another acceptable life pursuit?"

"Jennifer and David give them a whole new chance at an heir apparent. Though they wouldn't complain if I produced a few more."

Something changed in the timbre of Larry's voice. "You going to?"

"Maybe," said Crystal. She liked kids. And she could handle being both a mom and a writer. If she happened to find a man with a house and a good job, she could even move out of the apartment. "Know any guys who own real estate?"

"There are other options," he pointed out, watching Rufus drop the stick at his feet.

"Such as?"

"You could set aside a little each month, find a nice starter, a good mortgage broker."

"Is this going to be a math lecture, Professor Grosso?"

"More of a life lecture."

She pushed away from him, wading into the cool water until she was ankle deep. "Oh, no you don't. You're not ruining my weekend with practicality. Let's talk some more about sailing."

"You want to take a spin around the bay?"

"I'm talking about a fantasy. I see a thatched hut, palm trees, a bright cotton dress and two very large blender drinks."

"So, that's your fantasy?"

"That's my fantasy." She sidled back up to him, grinning playfully. "What's yours?"

His eyebrows went up. "You're joking, right?"

His gaze burned hers. Gold flecks appeared deep in his hazel eyes, burning bright and molten in the afternoon sun. He tilted his chin and cocked his head, leaning slightly in to engulf her in a wave of desire so strong her knees almost buckled.

Oh?

"Yeah," he answered her silent question.

She waggled her index finger back and forth between them just to be sure.

He nodded.

She swallowed.

He hesitated for a split second. "You okay with that?"

In answer, she came up on her toes and planted a heart-felt kiss on his mouth. She was completely okay with that, and overwhelmed that he'd been formal enough to ask.

He responded in under a second, his mouth opening, his arms going around her, while he dragged her flush against his body.

It was Rufus's bark that drove them apart. The dog deposited the wet stick at Larry's feet.

Larry quickly bent down and threw the driftwood stick in the direction of the beach house. Then he gazed at Crystal, eyes smoldering. "Race you back?"

She grinned and took off across the soft sand.

They made it to the staircase, breathing hard. Without

stopping, Larry scooped her up in his arms as if she weighed nothing at all.

Before she could protest, they were on the deck. He opened the glass door, let Rufus into the cool, quiet haven, then continued up the interior staircase, into the first bedroom in the hallway.

There, he slowed to a stop next to a massive, four-poster. He leaned in to kiss her, sliding her slowly along his body until her feet sank into the thick, cream-colored carpet. The bed had an emerald comforter and eight plump pillows, and the bay window was covered in lacy sheers. Burgundy and gold wallpaper panels were separated by strips of polished wood molding that matched the spires of the bed.

Larry slid the pad of his thumb along her jawline. "You are so incredibly beautiful," he breathed.

"Mathematically speaking?" she couldn't help but ask.

"Mathematically, artistically, scientifically. Come up with any benchmark in the world, you'll blow it out of the water."

Something inside her melted.

He cupped her cheek, slowly leaning forward, kissing her forehead, the tip of her nose. He touched his index finger to her chin, raising it, bending to her mouth. She strained toward him, and his lips engulfed her own once more.

She groaned at the exquisite sensation, and he pushed his outspread fingers into her hair, wrapping his other arm tightly around her body, anchoring her to him. She wound her arms around his neck, pressing her body tight against his strength.

His fingertips found a space between her shorts and her cropped T-shirt. They trailed along the exposed skin of her back, raising goose bumps and sending tingles of desire skittering up her spine.

She teased her tongue along his bottom lip.

He pressed her body more tightly into his, treating her to a kiss that made the fine hairs spring up on her forearms and her toes curl tight around the carpet fibers.

A shudder rushed through her, heat pooling in her stomach, her skin flushing hot in the streaming sunbeams. It was going to be so good. They were going to be so good together.

She waited.

"You absolutely sure about this?" he rasped.

In answer, she took a step back. She ripped her T-shirt over her head, tossing it on a nearby armchair, then walked back into his arms.

"One hundred percent," she whispered as her lips met his all over again.

She tangled her fingers in his hair, reveled in the taste of his mouth. He drew her into his arms, murmuring compliments all the while, and lowering her onto the deep mattress.

LARRY GAZED AT CRYSTAL across the table on the deck. The setting sun turned a few high clouds wispy pink, and the ocean was changing from bright-blue to gunmetal-gray. White foam still bubbled brightly on the sand, and a few people strolled by on the beach as the evening wind picked up speed.

But Crystal held his attention, legs curled beneath her in one of the deck chairs. They'd spent several hours in bed, making love, then napping, then making love all over again. He felt like a teenager. When hunger had finally roused them, she'd co-opted his navy-blue T-shirt, dragging it over her tousled hair while he called the local grocery store for delivery.

Now, she was munching on a lemon tart, licking the meringue from her fingers. He'd intended the tarts for dessert, but he wasn't about to complain about her idiosyncrasies. He couldn't believe this gorgeous creature had been in his bed. She was everything any man could possibly want: sweet, sexy, funny and smart.

"You're not hungry?" she asked, pushing the plastic container of lemon tarts toward him.

"I'm saving mine for dessert," he answered.

"You're much too traditional."

"That's not what you said an hour ago."

She grinned like a Cheshire cat, and pushed the tart package closer to him. "Go ahead, Professor. Live on the wild side."

He gave into her beguiling smile, lifting a tart to his mouth. "You know," he told her before biting into the flakey pastry and the tangy sweet filling, "There's this thing called Chaos Theory."

She waited, green eyes wide with expectation.

He swallowed. "It reminds me of you."

"This doesn't sound good."

Oh, it was good. It was intriguingly, amazingly good in this instance. "In part," he continued, "it's when the tiniest shift, over time, results in a massive change. And the seemingly chaotic reactions that follow are actually pre-ordained."

"You lost me," she admitted, but stretched across the table to snag another tart.

"When you climbed out of that parts delivery truck in Charlotte, despite the astronomical odds stacked against it, I believe I was pre-ordained to eat lemon tarts before dinner."

A slow smiled grew on her face, and she bit sexily into

the second tart. "Where I believe we were pre-ordained to end up in bed together. The tarts were entirely optional."

Larry matched her grin. "I'll give that one some thought."

"Do that. In the meantime, this girl doesn't survive on dessert alone."

"You're looking for a steak?" he guessed.

"I am. And some of that wine you keep bragging about."

He rose from his chair and retrieved a fork to check on the potatoes baking on the grill.

A few seconds later, Crystal sidled up behind him, her arms went around his waist, and she laid her cheek against his back.

He covered her hands. "I seem to recall something about you doing the cooking," he teased.

"Apparently," she responded with a happy sigh, "I'm unreliable."

"You think any self-respecting teacher would let you get away with that lame excuse?"

"You will," she assured him. And then she paused. "Because I'm naked under your shirt."

"That'll do it," he admitted.

She disentangled herself while he unwrapped the filet mignon. He seared them on the grill and added a combination of spices.

He thought he was the luckiest man on earth, as they dined al fresco at the glass table, while the sky turned to midnight purple and a quarter moon rose above the distant horizon.

CHAPTER SEVEN

THE NEXT DAY AT THE RACE track at Dover, Larry was torn between puffing his chest out to strut and keeping a respectful distance between him and Crystal. As they crossed the walkover bridge to the infield area, she twined her arm around his, and there was no denying it felt good. She was a gorgeous woman, and more than a few male heads turned admiringly her way as they ambled toward the garage area.

She was wearing a pair of beige slacks and a simple, pale-yellow top. Her shoes were low, but her legs were long and shapely enough that she didn't need the boost of heels. She'd pulled her hair into a ponytail, then tugged it through the back of a tan baseball cap, anchoring the hat to her head. Her earrings were simple gold studs, her other jewelry nonexistent. But it didn't matter. She still looked like that model who'd somehow wandered off that Paris runway.

Then he spotted his nephew Kent and crew chief Neil Sanchez coming the other way, their heads bent in an intense discussion. He smoothly and quickly disentangled his arm from Crystal and put some distance between them.

"Hey, Kent," he said, nodding. "Good luck today." Larry knew his son Steve wouldn't be spotting for Kent at the Dover race because of the suspension last week. But, distracted by his reunion with his fiancée, Heidi, Steve was handling the disappointment very well. Larry had talked to Steve during the week, offering advice where he could. After a breakup over Kent's sponsor and the NASCAR lifestyle, shortly after becoming engaged, Steve and Heidi were both so angry that it took all of the Grosso clan to help straighten it out. Larry was extremely happy that his son was back on track.

Kent glanced up and blinked Larry into focus.

"Oh. Hi, Larry." Kent's gaze slid briefly to Crystal, but he didn't seem to recognize her.

"Hi, Larry," Neil offered, but there was a tightness around his mouth as the two men kept walking.

"What are you doing?" Crystal asked Larry.

"What do you mean?"

"I've never had a man embarrassed to be seen with me before."

"I'm not embarrassed to be seen with you." The mere thought was ludicrous.

She gestured back to Kent and Neil. "Then what the hell was that all about?"

Larry pretended to misunderstand. "You think they were arguing?"

"Don't play dumb with me."

"Seriously," said Larry. "I think they were fighting about something."

"You're going to be fighting about something in a minute if you don't smarten up."

Larry tried to lighten the mood. "You're telling a rocket scientist to smarten up?"

"I am when he's behaving like a moron."

He sighed, knowing full well she was talking about how he'd distanced himself from her when he saw familiar faces. "I was trying to be discreet. There's no need to start gossip."

"I don't care about gossip."

"Well, you should. NASCAR is a tight-knit community."

"Is this an age thing?"

"This is an 'I don't want to announce our private business to the world' thing."

Her lips compressed. "You were perfectly fine until Kent came along."

"We were an anonymous couple until Kent came along."

"So, we're going to have a secret affair. Is that it?"

No, that wasn't it. Of course he didn't want a secret affair. He didn't want an affair at all. Trouble was, until he figured out exactly what was going on between him and Crystal, he didn't know how to present it to the world— or his family.

"Because I can be discreet," she told him, taking a backward step away from him. "I can be so discreet, you won't even know I'm here."

"Crystal."

She took a second step, and said, in a voice low and intense, "You want to hide me out at some beach house at night then pretend not to know me during the day—"

"Stop!" He hadn't meant to hurt her feelings. He took the two strides that separated them. "I want this to be dignified."

"It is dignified. Or at least it was until two minutes ago."

He lifted off his cap and dragged a hand through his hair. "You want to tell people we're dating?"

"Is that what we're doing?"

"See?" he hissed. "*We* don't even know what to call it."

"Do we have to give it a label?"

"If we don't, they will."

"So, let them."

"Are you serious?" Did she know what kind of speculation that would cause?

"Oh look," she said, nodding over his shoulder. "There's Dean and Patsy."

Larry twisted his head around.

"Hi, Dean. Hi, Patsy," Crystal called with a wave.

Then, before Larry could react, she snagged his arm, pulled herself up and gave him a nuzzling kiss in the crook of his neck.

His body clenched in horror.

"Speculate *that*," she muttered under her breath.

"I don't believe you did that," he growled, shaking free as he turned to meet his brother and sister-in-law.

Dean's eyes narrowed in suspicion.

Patsy's were wide with surprise.

"Crystal," she said. "I didn't expect to see you this far from Charlotte."

"Larry invited me," said Crystal, and Larry tensed, waiting to see what other information she was about to offer up.

"We've been discussing a writing project I'm working on," she finished.

"What project is that?" asked Dean, eyeing Larry up and down.

"A cookbook," Crystal supplied. "I saw you had a good race in Charlotte," she said to Dean.

Eyes still hard, Dean opened his mouth.

"Thank you," Patsy put in, forestalling whatever it was Dean had been about to say, and earning a scowl from her husband. "The charity walk went well this morning," she continued, directing her attention to Crystal. "I understand Softco made a nice donation."

"Missed you there," Dean said to Larry, innuendo sharp in his tone.

"I'll be sending a check," Larry added, refusing to rise to his brother's bait.

"So what were the two of—"

Patsy nudged her husband with her shoulder, talking overtop of him. "Will you be joining me in the motor home later?"

"We might head up to Alan Cargill's skybox," Larry offered, feeling Crystal's immediate and disapproving glare. "It's a little hot down here. Hope you don't mind but we dropped off Crystal's dog at your motor home."

"That's fine. It's the best place for him," Patsy said. "Well, we'd better get going. We don't want to be late for the driver introductions."

"Have a good race," Larry said to Dean, offering his hand.

"Good luck," Crystal echoed.

"Thanks," said Dean with a shake, but his expression told Larry they'd be talking later.

Larry watched them melt into the crowd. "See what I mean?" he said to Crystal.

"Are we going to hide up in the sky box and pretend we're just friends?"

He thought about that. "Maybe." Couldn't hurt. At least for a while.

"You plan to see me again?" She leaned her shoulder to his, tipping up to whisper in his ear. "You plan to sleep with me again?"

He couldn't deny that. "Absolutely."

"What are the odds we can keep it a secret?"

"I'd have to write an algorithm to know for sure."

"Ballpark it."

"You trying to beat me at my own game?"

"You bet."

He gave in with a harsh sigh. She was right. If they spent any amount of time together, their relationship was going to become public knowledge, at the very least public speculation. Hiding was a bad plan.

"Fine." He agreed, deciding they should ease people into the idea. "We can wander around the infield. We can hold hands. But no public kissing. We're not teenagers, and there are members of the press around here. As you know, the press loves my famous family."

"I'll try to restrain myself," she muttered.

He held back a smile. "You do that."

"But we're kissing later."

"Of course."

"I don't care if we have to park the rental car behind a warehouse or hide out in an airport restroom."

"I'm not going into the ladies' room. And you're damn sure not going into the men's room."

"Do you academics get paid by the debate?"

"We do."

"It shows."

He took her hand. "Then explain to me why you keep winning."

CRYSTAL WATCHED WITH RISING excitement as Kent Grosso hurtled his No. 427 car toward the finish line, trying to pass his father who was in the lead. Three cars were vying for the top spot. Dean was barely holding on to the lead as they tucked into Turn Two. Dean's No. 414 car went high. Kent went low, and the third car struggled to find an opening in the middle.

The checkered flag was out, and she gripped Larry's hand tightly as the announcer's voice rose with excitement. The crowd was on its feet and the spectators on the infield crowded the fence, while the cars hurtled down the straightaway.

She held her breath as the three contenders drove into Turn Three. Dean held on, held on, held on.

He made it out of the turn, sticking solidly to the race track as he covered the final stretch to the line.

"And he does it!" shouted the announcer as a hundred and fifty thousand spectators filled the air with cheers. "Dean Grosso hangs on to take the checkered flag and win the race."

Crystal whooped out a cheer and threw her arms around Larry. He hugged her tight, lifting her right off the ground.

"What a race," she breathed. "Dean first and Kent second."

Larry gave her a peck on the cheek, proud of his nephew. "When it comes together, it comes together."

"Are you sorry Steve wasn't spotting?" she asked, while Larry lowered her back to the ground.

The remaining cars whined past the start/finish line while Dean did a celebratory burnout to the roaring delight of the capacity crowd.

"He screwed up last week. No getting around that. He knows enough to be a man about it. Besides—" Larry gave her a wry smile "—I suspect Heidi's doing a bang-up job of consoling him. And his team did get the points. The Chase is coming up fast."

"And the points count above everything else," Crystal agreed.

"You've got the picture," said Larry. "Victory Lane?"

"You bet." She fell into step beside him as they followed the surge of the crowd.

By the time they grew close enough to see the action

at Victory Lane, Dean was climbing out of the race car, donning a Smoothtone Music hat. Team members clapped him in a hug as he was handed the trophy, which he hoisted in the air.

The Maximus Motorsports team had surrounded Victory Lane, and they were all grinning ear to ear.

"I should go congratulate the team," Larry shouted in Crystal's ear, taking her arm to steer her in that direction.

"You go," she shouted back, disentangling.

"I'll introduce you," said Larry, obviously trying to make up for his earlier reluctance to acknowledge her.

But Crystal shook her head. "It's the team's moment. And we're not sure how they feel about me."

Larry's eyes narrowed. "I'm not embarrassed."

"I'll be right here when you get back."

He opened his mouth to argue.

"Go," she insisted with a little shove. "Celebrate with them for a bit."

"If you're sure." Larry took a couple of backward steps.

She gave him a nod, since there was no way her voice would be heard above the crowd. Then she watched him disappear, and her gaze shifted toward the team.

"Enjoying Larry's company?" came Patsy's voice directly beside her.

Crystal quickly turned to see the woman's knowing smirk.

"I'm glad Dean won today," Crystal offered.

Patsy beamed with pride. "Both of my boys. It's a good day." Both women glanced to the No. 414 car, where Dean was playfully spraying champagne on his team.

"But Dean's not getting any younger," Patsy continued, a flash of annoyance coloring her eyes.

"Is he thinking about—"

"Tell me about Larry," Patsy put in smoothly, the anger disappeared as fast as it had risen. She linked her arm with Crystal's and a twinkle came into her sky-blue eyes.

"He went over to congratulate the team," Crystal offered.

"That's not what I meant, and you know it."

Crystal blinked, hoping against hope that Patsy would back off.

"I meant," Patsy elaborated, "now that my husband isn't glaring daggers at the two of you, what's going on?"

Crystal chose her words carefully. "We're getting to know each other."

"And how's that going?"

"It's going well," said Crystal, her gaze involuntarily falling on Larry where he was shaking a crew member's hand. He pulled another one back into a back-slapping hug.

"I sense a certain—" Patsy paused, waving a descriptive hand through the air "—*energy* between the two of you."

Crystal held a quick mental debate with herself. She and Patsy weren't exactly friends. But she had seen the woman on and off for most of her life, and she certainly trusted her.

"We're trying to keep it low-key," she finally offered.

"Why?"

"Larry's self-conscious."

"Libby's been gone for three years."

"It's the age thing."

"Ironic," Patsy offered with a grimace.

"How do you mean?"

"One brother thinks he's on the shelf, the other refuses to accept his own mortality."

"You'd like Dean to retire?" Crystal guessed. The

rumors had been flying fast and furious within the NASCAR world. Dean refused to admit this was his last season, but there was speculation none the less.

"I've begged him to retire," said Patsy. "Wisdom and experience will only get you so far. It also takes strength and agility to stay out of the wall."

Crystal privately acknowledged there was nothing in the world wrong with Larry's strength and agility.

"What?" prompted Patsy.

"Huh?" Crystal asked in return, embarrassed by the wayward direction of her thoughts.

"Something made you smile."

"It's nothing."

"Seems like a pretty entertaining nothing."

"Just remembering something that happened this morning."

"Fair enough," said Patsy. "I'll back off. I'm just grateful you're making Larry so happy. He looks so relaxed. Almost as if…" Patsy's eyes widened, and her mouth formed a perfect O.

Crystal felt her face heat up.

"You didn't," said Patsy, leaning in, in an obvious effort to keep the conversation private.

"I don't know what you're talking about," Crystal said.

"Never mind." Patsy waved away her words. "Don't tell me. None of my business." Then her gaze strayed to Larry. "But, you *did*."

"Patsy—"

"Well, thank goodness."

Crystal's brows shot up.

"The man needed something to get him back in the swing."

"Oh, he's back in the swing," Crystal admitted.

Patsy's grin grew wide.

"I can't believe I said that."

Patsy's hand came down comfortingly on Crystal's shoulder. "Your secret's safe with me."

"It just, kind of…" Crystal watched Larry joking in the midst of the chaos. "…happened," Crystal finished, thinking Larry was, by far, the sexiest man at the race track.

Patsy was silent, and when Crystal glanced at her, she looked pensive. Maybe she wasn't as supportive of the relationship as she pretended. In which case, Crystal might have done Larry a disservice by her admission.

"Something wrong?" she asked Patsy.

The woman gave her head a little shake and pasted on a smile. "Nothing at all."

"Seriously," said Crystal, looking closer, deciding it had to be something more serious than Patsy's brother-in-law's love life. It occurred to Crystal that Dean might have some kind of health problem. Maybe it was something that could compromise his ability to race. And maybe she should mind her own business. "I didn't mean to pry," she told Patsy apologetically.

But Patsy laughed. "Two minutes ago, we were discussing your sex life with my brother-in-law. I don't know how it gets too personal after that."

"Is Dean okay?"

A moment passed.

"There's nothing worse than a twenty-five-year-old man in a forty-nine-year-old body."

Just then, Dean emerged in Victory Lane, pulling his son into an enthusiastic hug.

"He obviously loves the sport," said Crystal.

"And I'd love him just as much in any other career."

Crystal's heart went out to the woman. "You're really worried, aren't you?"

Patsy nodded. "Every single time he straps into that car and puts on his helmet." She paused. "It didn't used to be like this."

"Have you talked to him about it?" asked Crystal.

"Until I'm blue in the face. I'm so—" Her voice broke. "Sorry."

Crystal wrapped an arm around her shoulders, tipping her head close to Patsy's. "Don't be sorry. You love him."

"I'm afraid," Patsy confessed, "that his reflexes aren't what they used to be. He thinks he's immune to aging, and the win today supports that."

"The sport is safer than ever," Crystal tried.

"I know every safety feature, every precaution. But they're still going 180 miles an hour."

It was true. Even with harnesses, helmets, roll cages and fire protection, there were still risks.

"Experience doesn't change the laws of physics," Patsy finished on a bitter note.

"*Mom*," came Kent's shout of joy as he emerged from the Victory Lane crowd.

He rushed forward, lifting Patsy into a tight hug and spinning her around.

Her face instantly lit up. "Way to go, sweetheart." She hugged him tight.

Crystal backed off a step or two, watching Dean join his family. Patsy saw him and immediately hugged him, all worrying pushed aside by love.

"Sorry I took so long," came Larry's deep voice next to Crystal's ear.

Something inside her instantly relaxed. "No problem. They look pretty excited."

"It was well earned."

"What now?" asked Crystal as more team members joined Kent and his parents.

"Well, we only had the beach house for one night," said Larry.

"So, that's out," Crystal agreed.

"A motel on the Interstate?" he playfully suggested, taking her hand and leading her through the crowd toward the exit.

"We'd miss our plane."

"Good point. Your place when we get back?"

Crystal cringed. "My parents have a key, and they've been known to randomly drop in."

"Ouch," said Larry.

"Um-hmm," Crystal agreed, shifting closer to him as the press of bodies closed in.

"This been a problem before?"

She nudged him in the ribs with her elbow. "None of your business. But no, it hasn't been a problem before. I only moved into the apartment after Simon died."

"Two *years?*"

"Got a problem with that?" She was willing to bet he hadn't been sexually active since his wife's death.

"No. But…" He eyed her up and down. "I know you don't like hearing this, but you're drop-dead gorgeous."

"That means I should be promiscuous?"

"You're an adult, Crystal. It's not promiscuous to have a healthy sex life."

"And there's nothing wrong with being particular, either."

Larry shifted her in front of him as they climbed the stairs to the walk over the bridge. At the top, he leaned forward to speak in her ear. "I have no idea why we're having this argument. What I meant to say was, 'good for you. You have every right to be particular, and I'm *glad* you were particular.'" A teasing note came into his voice. "Right up until me, of course."

"Yeah," she drawled. "I was obviously feeling charitable last night."

He moved up beside her as the crowd on the other side of the bridge thinned out. "And what about now? How are you feeling now?"

"Charitable," she confirmed with a nod. "Extremely and completely charitable. Your place?"

There was silence.

She glanced at his profile. "What?"

He breathed out a sigh. "Libby's bed."

Crystal squeezed her eyes shut for a second, regretting her stupidity.

"Maybe that's silly," he offered.

She wrapped her hand around his upper arm. "It's not silly at all. It's sweet and respectful."

They passed the concessions, heading for Dean's motor home to pick up Rufus.

Larry snaked an arm around her shoulders and tugged her close. "But I have another idea."

"That's what I love about a rocket scientist, always thinking."

"Ever been to Myrtle Pond?"

CRYSTAL DIDN'T KNOW WHICH surprised her more, that Larry owned a ramshackle, old Victorian home at Myrtle Pond or that he piloted a plane. They'd picked up his Cessna at the Charlotte airport. Then, after flying twenty minutes and passing low over a small, picturesque lake, with the pattern of varying size homes on the eastern shore, Larry had landed the plane on a gravel airstrip about a mile from the general store and gas station.

A big man in a plaid flannel shirt had met them in an old, battered pickup truck. He'd introduced himself as Nash Walkins, bait-shop owner.

So, squashed in the middle of the bench seat, wrinkling her nose at the faint odor of trout, Crystal had bounced down the rutted road to Larry's house.

"It needs a bit of work," said Larry as they rocked to a halt between the wide front porch and an overgrown lawn that swept down to an aging dock at the lakeshore. The sun was a dying orange ball, slipping fast behind the rolling hills on the far side of the lake.

Nash guffawed from the driver's seat.

"Okay, *quite* a bit of work," Larry amended.

White paint was peeling on the pillars and latticework. The shingles curled up from a bowed porch roof. And two of the front windows were covered in plywood.

"It's lovely," said Crystal, stretching the truth to within an inch of its life.

"She's a keeper," said Nash, with a nod at Crystal.

"She recognizes a diamond in the rough," said Larry.

"Actually," Crystal admitted, "I was just being polite." Nash laughed.

"You wait," said Larry. "We're going to restore it using Fibonacci numbers."

Crystal blinked her confusion at him.

"It'll be gorgeous," he finished.

"And for now?" she asked, gazing worriedly at the sagging door. Surely they weren't actually sleeping here.

"The electricity works. So does the plumbing," said Larry, creaking open the truck door.

"Upstairs only, for water," Nash warned.

"That's all we need." Larry swung out of the vehicle. "The café open?"

"It's Sunday," said Nash, exiting from the driver's side.

Crystal slid across the velour seat cover. "What does that mean?"

"The café's closed Sundays. We can grill some burgers on my deck," Nash offered.

Larry nodded. "Sounds good. I'll bring the wine."

Standing on the uneven ground, Crystal put her hands on her hips and stared up at the three story monstrosity. "I feel like a teenager in a horror movie."

Larry snagged her hand, pulling her against his side. "Don't worry," he muttered, then leaned down and planted a long kiss on her surprised mouth, leaving her speechless. "I'll keep you safe."

"You *sure* she doesn't have a sister available?" asked Nash.

"I'm working on it," Crystal answered. She'd like nothing better than for Amber to become available.

"Find your own dates," Larry growled at Nash. "He's a hound dog," he added for Crystal's benefit.

"You have a job?" she asked Nash.

"Own my own business."

"Then you've got my vote."

"It's a bait shop," Larry reminded her.

Nash folded his thick arms over his broad chest. "Nitroworms and night crawlers," he proudly informed her.

Crystal shuddered.

"See what I mean?" asked Larry, pulling down the tailgate so that Rufus could jump out of the box.

"Better to sell night crawlers than to be one," she pointed out. Though she honestly didn't think she could be intimate with a man who handled creepy crawly things all day long. But maybe Amber was different. Crystal would think about that.

"Need anything else?" asked Nash, his tone going serious.

Larry shook his head, settling their two overnight bags on his shoulder. "Half an hour?"

"See you then," said Nash, easing back into the driver's seat and slamming the door. The diesel engine roared to life.

"We're really sleeping here?" asked Crystal.

"The master bedroom is comfy. Honest."

She took a breath. "Whatever you say."

He started up the rickety stairs, and she followed along. "We'll have complete privacy."

Okay. That sounded pretty good.

Rufus sniffed at an old porch swing, glancing at Larry before gracefully leaping up to settle on the cushion. The springs creaked gently under his weight.

Larry shouldered open the door and hit a light switch.

The entry hall and living room were a jumble of power tools and building supplies. From what she could see, the dining room was the same, except its walls had been torn down, the bare two-by-fours exposed beneath.

"This way," said Larry, leading a winding path through rubble and plywood to a sweeping staircase.

It squeaked when he put his foot on the bottom stair.

"Is this thing going to collapse?"

He started up, tugging her along. "Trust me. I'm a rocket scientist."

"I'd feel better if you were a carpenter."

The worn banister wobbled under her hand. But before any real panic could set in, they were in the upstairs hallway. Larry pushed a door open, flicked the light on and motioned her into an astonishingly beautiful room.

The walls were copper in color, highlighting a polished cherrywood dresser, armoire, headboard and footboard. A cream-colored loveseat was positioned in one corner, across from two French provincial armchairs. On three windows in the corner room, pale gold curtains were held back by gleaming cords. Three tiffany-look lamps glowed on the dresser and bedside tables, reflecting off the patterned rug.

"Wow," she breathed.

"The former owner did this," Larry told her, moving to the windows to pull down the shades. "I suspect she had plans for the rest of the house. But she had a sudden financial setback."

Crystal moved into the room, running her fingers over the smooth surface of the dresser.

"Unfortunately," Larry continued, "there are structural problems underneath."

She couldn't help but glance worriedly at the floor.

"It won't fall apart tonight," he assured her.

"You sure about that."

He took her hand, drawing her into his arms. "Have a little faith, sweetheart."

She tipped her head to gaze into his warm eyes. "How long did you tell Nash we'd be?"

Larry glanced at his watch. "We have seventeen minutes."

Warmth swirling in her stomach, Crystal came up on her toes and kissed him. "I wish you'd made that a little longer."

CHAPTER EIGHT

RECOVERING FROM THE LONGEST, most passionate kiss in history, Crystal scrambled to comb out her mussed ponytail and fix her smeared lipstick, while Larry retrieved a couple of bottles of wine.

She straightened her top and smoothed the front of her pants, stuffing her feet back into her shoes.

"The world won't stop turning if we're five minutes late," he pointed out.

"But Nash will get suspicious."

"So what?"

"So, I thought we were trying to be discreet."

"I'm pretty much over that."

She paused on the way out the door. "Yeah?"

"Yeah. I guess if you're willing to be seen with me in public, I can handle being seen with you."

She started back down the stairs. "How truly magnanimous of you."

He followed behind. "Isn't it though?"

They exited through the front door.

Rufus opened one eye to watch them leave the porch. But then he sighed and closed it again as they headed down the dirt path to Nash's house.

The trees closed in around them. The light from Larry's porch faded, while Nash's house lights brightened in the distance. On the starlit pathway, Larry casually slipped his hand over hers. She was instantly filled with a sense of comfort and security.

She glanced up at his profile.

He reacted by looking down as they walked. "What?"

"I don't know," she answered honestly.

He slowed to a stop, turning to meet her eyes, his tone low. "But it's something, isn't it?"

She agreed with a nod. "It's something."

He leaned down to kiss her gently on the lips. "You're an amazing woman, Crystal Hayes."

"You're not so bad yourself, Larry Grosso."

She saw him smile.

"Later?" he asked.

"Absolutely."

He gave her hand a squeeze, and they continued down the pathway.

Nash was standing on his massive cedar deck, spatula in hand, burgers sizzling on the grill. Pot lights decorated his lush lawn, while overhead beams glowed burnished amber against the polished wood.

He nodded toward the open glass doors. "Beer in the fridge, or there's a corkscrew on the counter."

"You have a gorgeous home," said Crystal, gazing in awe at the ultra modern kitchen and the sparkling pool and hot tub combination off the far edge of the deck.

"Thank you," said Nash.

"He uses it to seduce women," said Larry, heading through the door with the wine.

"I imagine it works quite well," said Crystal.

Nash grinned unrepentantly.

"You probably want to stay away from my sister," Crystal joked.

"I wouldn't go near a woman who didn't know the score," Nash assured her.

Crystal's gaze slid to Larry as he opened the wine. Did Larry think *she* knew the score? Had he concluded—like so many men in the world—that she took sex casually?

The vibes she was getting from him felt sincere. But maybe it was all part of a game. And maybe he thought she was playing along.

He looked up, met her eyes and smiled. "Red or white?" he called.

"White, please," she answered, the intimate smile reassuring.

"Grab me a beer?" asked Nash, closing the lid on the propane grill.

Larry stepped out of the kitchen, a glass of red and one of white dangling from the fingers of one hand. In the other, he held Nash's beer. He handed them each their drink. Then he gestured to a cushioned love seat grouped with a couple of chairs around a low oblong table.

Nash turned out to be a marvelous cook. He produced gourmet burgers with salsa and avocado on homemade multigrain buns.

He'd only lived on Myrtle Pond for two years. Like Larry, he'd bought an aging house and rebuilt.

Crystal tried to press him for details of his life before the bait shop, but he was vague, other than to say he was an architect who'd given up the rat race. He clearly enjoyed having Larry as a new neighbor, and the men engaged in several good-natured arguments about the best way to redesign Larry's Victorian.

Mostly, Crystal got lost in the detail.

Around midnight, her cell phone rang. Surprised, she

extracted it from her handbag, trying to figure out who might call so late.

"It's Amber," she said to Larry, noting her sister's number with a sigh of frustration.

She flipped open the phone. "Hello?"

"Auntie Crystal?"

Crystal came alert, sitting up straight with shock at the sound of her niece's voice. "Jennifer? What's wrong."

Jennifer sniffed. "Mommy's not home yet."

"Are you *alone?*" Damn Amber. Damn her. Damn her. Larry came to his feet.

"Lisa Beechman's babysitting."

"Who's Lisa Beechman? Where's David?"

"David's in bed. Lisa says she has to go home now. She's really mad. I tried and tried Mommy's number." Jennifer's voice broke, and Crystal's heart squeezed tight.

"Honey, can I talk to Lisa?"

Nash was silent, while Larry was giving her a *what's up?* look.

"I'll go and get her," said Jennifer in a small voice.

Crystal covered the mouthpiece. "Amber's out, and the babysitter has to leave."

Larry glanced at his watch.

Nash stood. "I'll get the truck and tell Hank to turn on the runway lights."

"Thanks," said Larry.

"Hello?" came a clearly annoyed girl's voice on the other end of the line.

"Lisa? This is Jennifer's Aunt Crystal. Do you know where Amber went?"

There was a chopped sigh. "Somewhere with that guy."

"Zane?"

"Yeah. I guess. She promised she'd be back by ten. I have to work tomorrow, and there's no way—"

"Can you hang on for another…" Crystal glanced at Larry.

"Forty-five minutes," he said.

"Forty-five minutes?" Crystal finished.

"Isn't there anyone closer?"

Crystal thought of her mother, but her parents would be asleep. It would take them half an hour to get there. And she could well imagine the family turmoil if she brought her parents into the middle of this one.

"It's the best I can do," she told Lisa. "I'm really sorry. We're coming in by plane, but we're all the way out at Myrtle Pond."

The young girl heaved another sigh.

"I'll pay you double," Crystal offered.

"I guess," said Lisa. "It's not like I'm gonna walk out on two little kids."

Unlike their own mother, came Crystal's immediate and uncharitable thought.

"I'll be there just as soon as I can," she pledged. "Can I talk to Jennifer again?"

"Just a sec."

Larry took Crystal's hand, urging her to her feet and pointing to where Nash had the truck running.

"We'll get our stuff later," he told her as they started down the deck stairs.

"Hello?" came Jennifer's little voice.

"Hi, honey. Did your dad come back?"

"Yes," said Jennifer in a small voice.

"I'm on my way over so that Lisa can go home."

"'Kay," said Jennifer.

"Can you hang on for just a little while?"

"Uh-huh."

Larry boosted Crystal into the truck, and she slid across the seat to make room for him beside her.

Nash put Rufus in the back and, once in the truck, he pulled it into gear.

"Is David asleep?" asked Crystal.

"I think so," said Jennifer.

"Can you check? Can you make sure he isn't having any bad dreams?"

"Okay."

"Thanks, honey. And I'll see you soon. I'll sleep there tonight, then it won't matter how late your mommy gets home."

"Will you come and tuck me in?"

"Of course, I'll tuck you in. I'll give you a big old hug and a smoochie kiss."

"I might be in David's room."

"Then I'll find you there."

"I might be asleep."

"I'll hug you anyway."

"'Kay."

"You ready to say goodbye?"

"I guess."

"Okay. Goodbye, Jennifer. I'll see you soon."

"Bye, Auntie Crystal."

Crystal flipped the phone shut, silently cursing Amber's carelessness.

Larry stayed silent, but she could see his jaw was tense.

"My sister," she explained unnecessarily. "I guess she forgot about the time." Crystal waited for cutting words of condemnation against Amber.

"Then we better get you over there," Larry said simply. "Is Jennifer okay?"

"She sounded upset, but I think she's hanging in."

Gratitude rose in her chest for his matter-of-fact reaction to the problem.

Crystal's heart went out to her little niece. And though she wasn't admitting it out loud, she was furious with her sister. She was a mother, not just a party girl.

"Zane is back or he never left," she told Larry, watching the headlights bounce along the dark, rural road.

"So I gathered." His tone was grim.

"I'm guessing they're drunk," she admitted.

Larry nodded in the dim light from the dashboard.

"The important thing is Jennifer and David," she said out loud, more to herself than anyone else. She wanted to rail at Amber, but that would be unproductive at the moment.

Larry gave another nod.

"You're mad, aren't you?" she asked him.

He turned his head to look at her. "I wish there was somebody for me to be mad at. I don't know Amber, and I've never met Zane. None of this is your fault, and it damn sure isn't the children's."

"I ruined your evening."

His arm went around her shoulders. "Amber ruined yours."

"At least we'd already eaten the burgers," Nash offered.

Crystal couldn't help a small smile. "There is that."

"I take it your sister has a loser boyfriend."

"Ex-husband," Crystal said. "The father of her two children."

Nash nodded, fighting the potholes as he sped along the road to the airstrip.

"Thank you for driving us," said Crystal.

The big man shrugged. "I wish I could do more." He glanced over her head to Larry, some kind of silent message passing between the two men. "Anything else you need?"

"We're good," Larry responded.

"What's Zane's last name?" Nash asked.

The question surprised Crystal. "Crandell," she answered after a moment.

Nash nodded thoughtfully but didn't explain further as they came around a bend in the road. "Looks like Hank's got the lights on."

Larry gave Crystal a reassuring squeeze. "I'll have you back home very soon."

LARRY WASN'T IMPRESSED WITH Amber's apartment. It wasn't so much that the furniture was worn, the carpet patchy, or that smells of fish and beer wafted in from the hallway. What worried him were the unwashed dishes and the fast-food cartons littering the dining room table top.

He handed a fifty to the teenage girl who left to drive herself home.

"Amber is usually neater than this," said Crystal, gathering up the burger wrappers and cardboard cups.

"You don't have to apologize for your sister."

"I don't know what's wrong with her."

But Larry could tell by the expression on Crystal's face that she knew exactly what was wrong. Ex-husband Zane was wrong.

"Leave the mess," Larry told her. Amber needed to take the responsibility for herself.

Crystal crossed the galley kitchen and kicked open the door beneath the sink, depositing the trash. "I can't leave the mess. The kids need to eat breakfast here."

"We'll take them back to your place."

"Without asking Amber?"

Larry reluctantly conceded she had a point. He wasn't sure what the law would say about removing the children without their mother's permission. On the other hand, Amber had basically abandoned them, and Crystal was family.

"She's not usually like this," Crystal stressed, disappointment and frustration showing on her face. "They don't have a lot of money. But then neither do I."

He moved into the kitchen, taking her by the shoulders. "This isn't about money. It's about responsibility. You can't feed your kids fast food then take off partying half the night. Do you honestly think Amber will get up to make them breakfast?"

Something banged against the outer door. A key scraped the lock, while a woman's high voice giggled on the other side.

Larry turned, putting himself between Crystal and the doorway.

It yawned open.

A tall, blond, willowy woman's eyes went wide beneath her heavy mascara. "Who are—"

"It's me, Amber." Crystal stepped out to where her sister could see her. "Where've you been?"

Amber's expression turned defiant. She sauntered the rest of the way into the apartment, dropping a jeweled purse on the tattered table beside the door. A man appeared behind her, and Larry held his gaze for a long second.

He was thin and long limbed. His hair could have used a cut, and he sported a straggly goatee on pale, sallow skin. His eyes had the glaze of liquor and recreational drugs.

Neither of them spoke.

"Well?" Larry prompted. "Crystal's wondering where you've been."

"Out," said Amber, plopping down on the couch. "The Flambé Bar, the Harold Club. Oh, and the Buzz Bomb. That was a blast." She turned to Zane. "Wasn't it, baby?"

The man gave a slow, slick smile. "A blast."

Crystal elbowed her way past Larry. His instinct was to stop her, but he didn't want to overstep his bounds.

"You told Lisa you'd be home by ten."

Amber's fuzzy eyes narrowed in puzzlement, then they opened wider in comprehension. "Oh. You mean the babysitter?"

"Jennifer called me," said Crystal.

Amber waved a dismissive hand. "We were only a little bit late."

Zane moved forward. "Yeah. What's the big deal?"

Larry stepped forward, too, positioning himself behind Crystal. He placed his hands on her shoulders and stared at Zane. "Time for you to say good night."

Zane opened his mouth, but then apparently thought better of it. He leaned down to give Amber a slack kiss. "Later, babe."

She whirled her head around to look at him. "Will you call tomorrow?"

Larry felt Crystal tense beneath his hands.

"Yeah. Sure. Got some business to take care of in the morning." Zane shot Larry a smug look that said he was a freewheeling, high roller of an entrepreneur.

Larry took in his sad manicure and bargain basement shoes, and remained completely unimpressed.

Zane made a gun out of his thumb and forefinger, aiming it in Larry's direction before pulling the trigger. Larry supposed it was meant to intimidate, but Zane was the one walking away, so it came off as desperate and pathetic.

The door shut behind Zane, and Crystal immediately confronted her sister.

"You can't *do this,* Amber," she warned.

"Do what? Have a little fun? Party with my husband? I got a frickin' babysitter, didn't I?"

"You were almost three hours late coming home."

Amber sighed, and tipped her head back on the couch. "The band was awesome." Then she started humming a song.

"You want me to take the kids home with me?" asked Crystal.

Amber's head snapped up. "No. I don't want you to take *my* kids home with you. I'm here now."

"Will you feel like getting up in the morning?" Crystal tried.

"I'll be fine. The school is having sports day tomorrow, and David's going to a birthday party after that."

"Did you remember to buy a present?"

"Of course I remembered to buy a present. Who the hell died and made you the lifestyle police?"

"Crystal," Larry interrupted. "Didn't you promise Jennifer you'd say good night?"

Crystal stared at him for a moment, as if she'd just remembered he was there. Then she gave a nod and rose from her chair. "I'll be right back."

Larry waited until Crystal disappeared down the hall. Then perched on the edge of the chair she had abandoned.

"I'm Larry," he said, holding out his hand.

"Amber," Amber responded, suspiciously.

Larry nodded, glancing around thoughtfully. "Struggling to hold it all together, are you?"

She shrugged. "Been busy lately."

"With Zane?"

"Yes. With Zane."

Larry nodded again.

"What?" she asked sharply.

Larry decided there was no percentage in beating around the bush. Crystal did enough of that for both of them. He was going for broke.

"You can do better than him."

"Better than Zane?"

"A lot better. You have two kids to think about."

"Zane's their father."

"That doesn't mean he's good for you."

"How would you know? What makes you an expert on what's right for my kids? Two parents getting back together, that's what's right for my kids."

"Keeping you out three hours late isn't right."

"How do you know I didn't keep him out?" She plunked a throw pillow into her lap. "Maybe I don't want to be Mommy twenty-four seven. You have any kids?"

"I have a son."

She glanced pointedly at her watch. "Where is he now?"

"He's an adult."

"Where's his mother?"

Larry kept his voice even. This wasn't about him. "She died."

Crystal reappeared, and Amber glanced from Larry to Crystal and back again. "What's the story with you two?"

Crystal looked startled. "What do you mean?"

"I mean, why are you together at one in the morning?"

"We were on a date," said Larry.

"You don't think he's a little old?"

"Amber!"

Amber gestured at Larry. "Well, he's out here giving me a lecture on how I can do better than Zane. Maybe I think you can do better than Larry."

"I'm quite sure she can," Larry said quietly.

"I can't," said Crystal. "And I don't want to. And how the hell did this get to be any of your business?"

"You're in my house, talking about my relationship."

Crystal took a deep breath. "You'll get the kids to school tomorrow?"

Amber glared at her.

"Okay," said Crystal, moving toward the door.

Larry rose to go with her.

"You and Zane are your own business," Crystal conceded. "But if you go out with him again, you call me. I'll babysit. Anytime."

The anger went out of Amber's expression. "Thanks, sis."

"You'll call?"

"Of course." Her laughter tinkled lightly. "Why would I say no to free babysitting?"

Crystal glanced at Larry, knowing he was the one who had paid Lisa tonight. He gave her a subtle shake of his head. He had no desire to make an issue of it. Jennifer and David were great kids. He had no objection at all to kicking in for their care.

He and Crystal walked silently down the stairs and out onto the sidewalk where Rufus waited in the car.

"I really don't know what to say," she finally offered.

He hit the unlock button on the car, heading for the passenger side to open her door. "Neither do I," he told her honestly. "The weekend didn't exactly end the way I'd expected."

She coughed out a laugh. "It didn't turn out *anything* like I'd expected."

Larry smiled in return as he opened the door.

She paused partway in. "Want to do it again sometime?"

"All of it?" he asked, not bothering to mask the hope in his voice.

"Any and all," she replied.

"You busy next weekend?"

"Nope."

"You busy tomorrow night?"

She shook her head.

"What about now? You busy right now?"

She squeezed her eyes shut for a second. "I really have to sleep."

He smoothed back her hair. "Of course you do." It was one o'clock. And there was no good place for them to sleep together. He didn't want to take her to a motel.

Maybe he'd rearrange his house tomorrow, move his old bed into the guest room and buy a brand new one. He was single now, and it was time for him to make the space his own.

He shifted his hand so it was cupping her cheek, leaning down to give her a gentle kiss on the mouth. "Dinner at my place tomorrow?"

She drew back, giving him a questioning look.

"I want you to see it," he told her.

There were so many things he wanted to show her, to tell her, to discuss with her. He knew his emotions were running way too hot, but he couldn't seem to help himself. He was a revving engine, and she was nitrous oxide.

"Tomorrow," he promised.

"Love it," she responded with a smile.

CHAPTER NINE

AS CRYSTAL MUNCHED HER WAY through her morning cereal, she couldn't decide which to put on the top of her worry list: her sister, her niece and nephew, or her burgeoning feelings for Larry.

She'd spent the weekend with a man.

She'd made love with him, and she'd have done it again had the date not ended abruptly. He was fun and funny, attractive and intelligent. And his sex appeal was off the charts. The men in her future were going to have one heck of a time measuring up.

If there *were* any men in her future.

At the moment, she couldn't imagine herself with anyone other than Larry. Which led to an interesting question. Where did they go from here?

Since her disaster of a marriage with Simon, she hadn't thought much about the future with any individual man. She'd had a generic fantasy in the back of her mind of a husband and children, a picket fence and a dog.

Her gaze strayed to Rufus where he was snoring on the living-room mat. He wasn't what she'd pictured for the dog, but he was growing on her. And now she, astonishingly, had trouble imagining any other dog.

Just like she had trouble imagining any other man.

But Larry might not want more children. She knew

Dean was in his late forties, so Larry must be fairly close to the same age. She hadn't asked, because asking made it seem like it mattered, and it really didn't. Except when it came to the tricky question of children.

Steve was completely grown up. He had a great career. He was engaged and about to embark on his own life. Heck, Larry could become a grandfather in the next few years. Why would he want to become a new father?

And, really, why on earth was she obsessing about this? They'd slept together one time. They'd had, technically, three dates. And here she was planning their happily ever after. Larry would probably break out in hives if he had the slightest inkling of the direction her thoughts were taking.

There was a shuffling noise on her porch as somebody reached the top of the stairs.

Rufus's ears perked up, and Crystal rose in anticipation of a knock. Maybe it was Larry. And maybe she should wipe this stupid, dreamy expression off her face and behave like an adult.

"Crystal?" her mother called through the closed door.

"Hey, Mom." She quickly wiped the expression off as her mother turned the knob to enter.

"You coming down to work today?" her mother asked without preamble.

Crystal nodded. "Sure. Something going on?"

Stella closed the door behind her. She was dressed in no-nonsense charcoal slacks with a pale-blue, Softco Machine Works collared shirt tucked into the waistband. She'd always tended toward stocky, but she was solid and healthy and still full of energy, even though she was in her fifties.

"Just the usual," she said. Then her gaze went to Rufus,

and she wrinkled her nose. "I came up on Saturday, but it looked like you were away."

"I went to the race at Dover." No sense beating around the bush. Amber had met Larry last night, and word would be out in the family by the end of the week. "With Larry Grosso."

Her mother's expression tightened. "I thought he was helping you with your cookbook."

"We're also friends."

"Friends?"

"We like each other. We enjoy each other's company."

Stella's face pinched in suspicion, but she didn't voice the obvious question. "Your father and I wanted to talk to you."

Crystal's first thought was about Amber. Or maybe it was Larry. Then she had the horrible thought that one of her parents could be ill.

"Is everything okay?"

"Pretty much," said Stella.

"What does *that* mean?"

"It means I want to talk to you later, with your father and Amber."

"Mom."

"You'll just have to be patient. This curiosity of yours has always been a problem."

"I'm not curious."

Her mother frowned at her.

Crystal wanted to press further, but Stella was as stubborn as they came. Stella wanted a family conference, and she'd wanted to pique Crystal's interest. She had.

"What time?"

"Six."

"For dinner?"

"Of course for dinner."

So much for her date with Larry. "Did Amber say yes?" On the bright side, at least it would keep Amber away from Zane tonight.

Then Crystal had another thought. "Are the kids coming?" She didn't want any more marginal babysitting situations.

"I haven't talked to Amber yet."

"Make sure she brings them."

Stella stared at her with a probing curiosity. But Crystal wasn't about to crack. She could play things equally close to the chest.

After her mother left, Crystal went straight to the phone, dialing Larry's number, which had mysteriously lodged itself in her brain. Funny, it usually took her weeks or months to memorize a number.

"Larry Grosso," came his clipped greeting.

"Larry, it's Crystal."

His tone immediately softened. "Hey, Crystal."

"Sorry to bother you."

"What makes you think it's a bother?"

She found herself unaccountably nervous. "Well, you weren't expecting me to call…"

"I love it when you call."

"You do?"

"Yes. What's up?"

She cleared her throat. "My mother just invited me for dinner tonight."

Silence.

"It's some kind of family conference. Something big, or at least big in her mind. Amber's invited, too."

"Then our date is off."

She sighed. "Afraid so."

He was silent again.

"I'm sorry," she quickly told him, putting all the sincerity she could muster into her voice. "*Really* sorry."

"How late will it go?" he asked.

"I don't know."

"Call me after?"

"Yeah?" She couldn't help the almost breathless tone of anticipation.

"Yeah," he assured her. "Call me as soon as you're done."

LARRY DIDN'T BELIEVE IN LUCK. He believed in hard, cold facts as proven out millions of times a day through the laws of physics and mathematics. But it sure seemed like fate was throwing a lot of roadblocks in his way when it came to Crystal. Given how anxious he was to spend time with her, and how interested she seemed in spending time with him, the law of averages said they should have gotten together more times than they'd managed so far.

If he was a superstitious man, he might be getting a little worried. But he wasn't, and he wouldn't, and he was going to finish redecorating the bedroom.

As usual, he'd been up since four. He'd hauled the guest bed down to the basement, moved Libby's brass bed into the guest room, and was busy reallocating her touches to the living room and dining room.

She'd loved watercolors, where he preferred oils. The mauve and pink floral painting that had hung above their bed was now at one end of the formal dining room. He'd taken a pair of seascapes from the living room and put them on the wall of the bedroom. He'd found a massive, dark oak four-poster in an Internet catalogue this morning. It was being delivered from a local store at noon.

Libby had chosen a French provincial loveseat for their bay window alcove. Larry was replacing it with a pair of hunter-green leather armchairs. The dressers were fine, but the doilies and cut glass perfume bottles could be put away. And right now, he was heading for the hardware store to find a light fixture that would suit his new vision of the room.

"Dad?" Steve's voice drifted up from the downstairs entry, and there was the sound of the front door closing behind him.

Larry quickly headed out of the master bedroom, hit with a sudden flash of guilt.

"On my way down," he called over the railing.

He trotted down the stairs to see his son in the entry hall in a blue golf shirt and a pair of navy slacks.

"Where's Heidi?" he asked, surprised to find Steve alone so soon after their romantic reunion.

"She's at the vet clinic." Steve frowned. "What's this I'm hearing about you and Crystal Hayes?"

Larry slowed to a stop at the bottom of the stairs. "What is it you're hearing?"

"That you spent this past weekend together."

"Where are you hearing that?"

Steve took a step forward. "What does it matter?"

"It matters a great deal. I don't like people gossiping about her."

"About *her?* That's what you're worried about? What about *you?*"

"What about me?"

"Are you having a midlife crisis?"

"What the hell kind of a question is that?"

"You want a sports car, Dad? Because I can get you a sports car."

"I don't want a sports car," Larry growled. He hated that his own son could write off his feelings as nothing more than some statistical hormone grasp at youth.

"You do know she's younger than *I* am," Steve accused.

No. Larry hadn't known that. Quite frankly, he'd been afraid to ask. It shouldn't surprise him. It didn't surprise him. But, damn, it would have been nice if she was a respectable thirty-five.

"I want to know who's gossiping about her," he told his son.

"Everybody."

"Well, *everybody* ought to get a life. We're friends. We've been on two or three dates."

"Dates?" Steve snorted his disbelief. "Uncle Dean thinks you're sleeping with her."

"My personal life is none of Uncle Dean's business."

"Are you sleeping with her?"

"My personal life is none of your business, either."

"I'll take that as a yes."

"Take it any way you want." Larry didn't need the third degree from his own son.

"Dad, you need someone your own age. This isn't going to end well. I'm worried about you."

Larry hadn't been thinking about it ending at all. As far as he was concerned, it had barely begun. Crystal was a beautiful, intelligent, incredibly sexy woman who seemed to enjoy his company. Why did that have to be a problem?

"You stop to think about what she's after?" asked Steve.

Larry glared at him.

"She has to know you have money."

"How the hell would she know that?" Larry didn't lead a flamboyant lifestyle. His investments were just that, investments.

Sure they'd done well. He was a mathematician after all. In his second year of graduate school, he'd written an algorithm to predict the stock market. It had worked. But nobody outside the family had any inkling he made any more than a college professor's salary.

Steve threw up his arms in frustration. "She researched you, Dad. You're a Grosso. We're one of NASCAR's first families."

"*I* approached her."

"The best cons always start that way."

Larry felt anger well up from the pit of his stomach. Crystal hadn't researched him. She wasn't after his money. She wouldn't even spend the money Simon left her, because she was too principled to touch it. She was one of the most honest, unselfish, honorable women he'd ever met.

His voice went cold. "I think you'd better leave."

Steve's jaw clenched tight. "You're in denial, Dad."

"I'm falling in love, Steve."

As he uttered the words, Larry knew they were true. Maybe it was wrong. Maybe it was too soon. Maybe the age difference was insurmountable. And maybe Crystal didn't return his feelings. But, there it was.

It was the reason he was putting Libby into perspective, into the past, in a sweet, warm corner of his heart where she'd stay forever.

"I can't believe this," Steve hissed. "Is it about sex? Is that it?"

"This conversation is over," said Larry.

"What are the odds?" Steve persisted. "You're a bloody mathematician. What are the odds she's in love with you—"

"I never said she was in love with me. I said I was in love with her."

"Well, at least you've got that part right."

"Goodbye, Steven." Larry crowded his son toward the door.

"Protect your assets, Dad."

"You don't know a single thing about her."

Steve put his hand on the doorknob. "Maybe not, but you can bet I'm going to find out."

"Don't do it."

Steve's gaze bore into his. "Afraid of what I might find out?"

"I'm afraid you might hurt Crystal."

"Dad." Steve's sigh was pleading.

"I'm an intelligent man, son."

"On paper, I know."

Larry drew back. What the hell did that mean?

"Your social IQ," said Steve. "It's…"

"Oh, don't stop now," Larry urged, his voice a low growl.

"You know social interaction's not your strong suit."

Maybe not in crowds, but it was perfectly fine with Crystal. "And you genuinely believe, through my social ineptitude, I'd let some gorgeous, young woman get her hooks in me?"

"You're only human, Dad. And you've been lonely since Mom died."

Larry paused for a moment. "You should meet her."

It was Steve's turn to draw back. "Bad idea."

"Afraid you might like her?"

"I'm afraid that's exactly what she wants. To insinuate herself into your family life."

Larry drew an exasperated sigh. "I hope you change your mind. Because I won't stop seeing her—not for you or anybody else."

Steve paused. "This could be an expensive lesson."

"I'm betting the lesson will be yours. I have good taste in women, Steve. I picked your mother, didn't I?"

"That was a long time ago."

A pain flicked across Larry's chest. But it was weaker than before, less sharp. He was sad now, not devastated like he'd been for so many months and years.

"It was," Larry agreed softly.

"Be careful, Dad," said Steve, genuine caring evident in his eyes.

"I will," Larry promised, feeling the fight go out of him. "See you at Pocono?"

Steve nodded, opening the door.

AMBER WAS LATE ARRIVING FOR dinner. But when the kids bounced through the front door, Crystal breathed a sigh of relief.

She was in the dining room with her mother, setting out stoneware plates and gold-tinted water glasses. Arms out, a whining engine noise sputtering from his lips, David rounded the brown, brocade couch, zipped past the magazine-covered oak coffee table and nearly careened into the china cabinet that straddled the dining room and living room.

"Hi, Grandma. Hi, Auntie Crystal."

"How are you, David?" asked Crystal, happy to see him looking more carefree. Maybe she was blowing the Zane situation out of proportion.

"I'm a fighter jet. One of the Blue Angels." And he was off through the kitchen and down the hall.

"We saw them on sports day," said Jennifer. "They were flying over the football stadium at State."

David appeared in the living room again. "They went straight up in the air," he whooped. "I'm going to be a jet pilot."

Crystal could almost hear Larry telling her there was a

lot of math in flying fighter jets. She glanced at her watch, then surreptitiously checked the stove, wondering how long it would be before dinner got started.

"Do I smell baked ham?" asked Amber, appearing in the dining room, a smile on her face. She looked a lot better than she had last night. Her eyes were clear, her hair was loose and freshly washed, and her makeup didn't look as harsh as it had last night.

"Grandma baked a chocolate cake!" Jennifer called from the kitchen.

"Did I forget a birthday?" asked Crystal, wondering why her mother was pulling out all the stops. At the same time, she felt a little guilty that her mind was wandering to Larry when her mother had gone to so much work.

Stella wasn't normally the Susie-homemaker type. She had a cleaning service on Fridays, usually offered cold cereal for breakfast, ate lunch at the local diner, and was known to pop frozen entrées in the microwave several times a week.

"Chocolate is your grandfather's favorite, Jennifer," said Stella.

Crystal caught Amber's eye, and they exchanged a curious look. Stella hadn't spent a lot of her life doing little things for their father, either. It was more the other way around.

Just then, Harold Hayes came in through the back door.

"And how are my girls?" he asked heartily.

"Grandpa!" Jennifer called, rushing to hug him.

David zoomed in from the hallway, arms still out like airplane wings. "I'm not a girl," he informed his grandfather.

Harold rustled his hair. "Of course you're not."

"I'm going to be a fighter jet pilot."

"Good for you."

"What's in your pocket, Grandpa?" Jennifer sang.

David bobbed his head up and down, eyes shining up at his grandfather.

Harold made a show of searching through the pockets of his work pants. "Let's see. Well, lookie here. Is that a…"

"What is it? What is it?" the children cried.

"Chocolate panda bear?"

"Our favorite! Thank you, Grandpa, thank you."

"After dinner," came Stella's warning voice.

"Can you put them beside your plates?" asked Harold.

Hands outstretched, the children eagerly nodded, and he handed them each a cellophane-wrapped chocolate panda.

They scampered to their usual chairs at the dining-room table.

"How are my big girls?" Harold asked Crystal and Amber, as he moved through the kitchen.

"Fine, Dad," said Crystal, giving him a peck on the cheek.

"Fine, Dad," Amber echoed. "How are you?"

"Feeling great," he beamed, giving Crystal yet another moment of confusion. Her father had always been the most easygoing of her parents. But he seemed almost unnaturally jovial tonight.

Maybe they had good news. A big contract? An expansion of the business? Or maybe they'd finally decided to redecorate the house. Her father had wanted to close in the garage for years. Her mother had insisted it was a waste of time and money.

"Will you open the wine now, Harold?" Stella's tone implied it wasn't really a question. "Crystal, the ham can be carved, and Amber can drain the vegetables. Kids, don't forget to wash up."

Within minutes, dinner was on the table and the dishes were being passed around. Amber filled the wineglasses, while Crystal made sure the children didn't drown their salads in dressing.

"Kenny Carmichael's son joined Softco as an apprentice," said Stella, referring to their shop foreman.

"He's old enough?" asked Crystal. Last time she'd seen Wesley Carmichael, he was in junior high.

"Graduated top of his class in pre-apprenticeship."

"That's great," said Crystal.

"Nice to have *some* young people interested in a good career," Stella harrumphed.

Warning flags went off in Crystal's head. Surely tonight wasn't going to be a lecture about her joining the company. She'd make a terrible machinist. And she sure wasn't going into sales or accounting.

"How are things at Wendals?" Harold asked Amber. Wendals was the discount ladies' clothing store chain where Amber was a shift supervisor.

"Good," said Amber with a nod, polishing off her glass of wine and reaching for the bottle.

Crystal automatically checked other people's glasses, finding most of them still full. She watched fatalistically as Amber refilled hers to the top.

"Mr. Laity is still being a jerk about holidays," said Amber. "And the new clerk is lazy, but at least they fixed the lunch-room fridge."

Her father's gaze went to Crystal. "And how's the book coming along?"

"Three more interviews to go," she told him. "I should see the cover design next month."

"Are you expecting any money from it?"

"Not much," she admitted. If she was lucky, it would pay out decently over the long term. But it wouldn't be the kind of royalties that paid the rent.

His lips compressed. "Hmm."

"At least she has Simon's pension and life insurance," her mother put in.

Crystal didn't say anything. Her parents had no idea she wasn't touching that money. If she told them, they'd ask why. And that would open up an entire can of worms.

Her parents exchanged a look.

"What's going on?" asked Crystal, glancing from one to the other.

Her mother took a deep breath. "Your father and I are selling the business."

Amber froze, wineglass halfway to her mouth.

Crystal gave her head a little shake, certain she couldn't have heard properly. "What business?"

"Softco, of course," said her mother. "Kenny and a group of investors made us an offer. And what with Wesley joining the team and all…"

Were they bluffing? Was this blackmail? Was it some kind of convoluted plot to get Crystal and Amber to become machinists?

Her parents would never sell Softco. It was their lifeblood. Without it, well, they barely had an identity. They didn't have interests or hobbies, or friends outside the Chamber of Commerce.

"Our lawyer is working out the details this week. There's a deposit in escrow, and—"

"Wait a minute," Crystal interrupted, setting down her knife and fork. "You're serious?"

Both her parents stared at her. "Of course we're serious."

"But—"

"We have our eye on a little bungalow in Florida," said Harold.

"You're retiring?" Crystal felt compelled to confirm, feeling as though something had just tilted the earth off its orbit.

Her family without Softco? It was almost incomprehensible. And what did that mean for her? She didn't want to get selfish, but would Kenny keep her on as a parts driver? Would he let her stay in the apartment?

"We're retiring," said her mother. "It's been a lot of years of hard work. We had high hopes for you girls, but since that doesn't appear to be—"

"What your mother means," her father put in, "is that now is a good time to sell. You girls don't want the business, so we're better off with other investments."

"What kind of investments?" asked Amber, her second wineglass now half empty.

"*Amber,*" Crystal jumped in. "That's none of our business."

Amber cocked her head, giving Crystal a glassy-eyed stare. "I'm just wondering what it means to us. Are we part of this windfall—"

"*Amber!*"

"Well, I've got kids to put through college."

"We'll be making provisions for their college educations," said Harold.

Amber gave her a saucy sneer, and Crystal wished she could crawl under the table.

"About this Florida house—" Crystal tried to steer the conversation away from Amber.

"What about now?" asked Amber. "The kids have needs now."

"Don't you mean Zane has needs now?" As soon as the words were out, Crystal regretted them.

"Zane?" asked her mother.

"Zane's back," Crystal said. "You can't give Amber any money while he's in town."

"I can't believe you just said that," Amber growled.

"Jennifer," Harold quickly put in, "Why don't you and David go into the den. I've got a new DVD there for you."

"Which one?" asked Jennifer.

"Can we take the chocolates?" asked David.

"You can take the chocolates," said Harold. "The movie is on top of the player. It's a surprise."

The kids jumped from their chairs and scampered down the hall.

Amber polished off her wine. "Zane's changed," she stated, with a frown for Crystal.

"There'll be some money in a trust for each of you," said her father.

A satisfied smile came over Amber's face, while Crystal's dinner turned to lead in her stomach. Amber would never get rid of Zane if there was money in the offing.

"You can access it when you're thirty-five," Stella finished.

Amber's face fell. "What good does it—"

"That's very generous of you," Crystal quickly put in, relieved on at least one front. On every other front, her life had just taken a hairpin turn.

CHAPTER TEN

IT WAS NINE-THIRTY BEFORE Larry's cell phone rang. He had the new bed set up in his bedroom, along with crisp new sheets and a copper-colored comforter that brought out the wood grains in the oak bed.

"Larry Grosso," he answered out of habit.

"Hey, Larry," came her sweet, melodic voice.

He smiled. He loved that voice. "Hey, Crystal."

"How're you doing?"

"Better now."

"Yeah?"

"Yeah."

"Dinner's over."

Great. "Where are you?"

"I'm in my car."

"On your way here, I hope?"

"I'm on Springford, crossing the overpass. Your directions are perfect."

"Where's Rufus?"

"He's with me."

"Good."

There was a thread of laughter in her tone. "You missed Rufus?"

"If he's here, we know he's fed and walked." They also knew Crystal wouldn't have to leave early. In fact, Crystal didn't have to leave at all.

Her voice was husky over the phone link. "You read my mind."

"Oh, I hope so."

"Be there in ten minutes."

He didn't want her to sign off. There was no reason they couldn't keep talking. "How was dinner?"

She gave a sigh.

"What?"

"My parents dropped a bombshell."

"Yeah?"

"They're selling the business."

"What business? Softco?"

"That's the same question I asked. Yes, they're selling Softco. They're moving to Florida."

Something twisted in Larry's chest. "You going with them?"

"No. I'm not going with them. I'm twenty-eight years old."

Damn. There it was. And it was worse than he'd thought. "You're only twenty-eight?"

"That's plenty old enough to leave my parents."

He paused. "Crystal?"

"Yes?"

"I'm fifty."

There was silence at her end, just the rumble of the motor and hum of the tires.

"I guess it's about time we stopped dancing around that," he said.

She still said nothing.

"You have a problem with it?" he asked.

"I'm still driving toward you. Why? You got a problem with it?"

"Yeah, I've got a big problem with being the luckiest guy on the planet."

"I'm turning onto Alder. The light's green. I'll be there in two minutes."

Larry's heartbeat deepened in anticipation. "Is Rufus going to need anything right away?"

"Not a thing."

"I bought a new bed," he told her. "Moved the old one into the guest room. Spent the whole day redecorating."

"For me?"

"For you."

"I'm passing number three-fifty," she told him.

"Can you see my car? Under the streetlight?"

"I see it. Three houses. Two."

Larry headed for the door and opened it. "I can see your headlights."

"I'm turning in."

"Watch out for the hedge." He heard a scraping sound.

"Wasn't crazy about that paint anyway," she told him.

He chuckled low. "Didn't sound too bad."

Her headlights died, and she shut off the engine.

Then she was opening the door. The interior glow backlit her hair. Her face was dark, but he could picture it in his mind. She was wearing a green tank top and a short, denim skirt.

She turned to open the back door.

"You're gorgeous," he breathed into the phone.

"So are you," she responded.

"You haven't seen me yet."

"But I remember."

"So do I," he rumbled. "So do I."

Rufus leapt out of the car, sniffing his way across the bark-mulch garden.

Larry called his name, closing the phone as Crystal strode toward him.

Rufus shot through the doorway, with Crystal right behind.

Larry closed and latched the door, pulling her into his arms and backing her into the entryway wall.

"I missed you," he whispered, framing her face with his palms.

She smiled, and he leaned in for a kiss.

Her lips were warm and sweet, malleable beneath his pressure. She snaked her arms around him and tipped her head sideways.

One of his arms went around her waist, then he smoothed her eyebrow, stroked the slope of her nose, her soft cheek, her chin, and he ran the pad of his thumb over her bottom lip. "Twenty-eight, eh?"

"Get over it."

He scooped her into his arms. "I intend to try very, very hard to do just that."

She laughed as he swept her up the stairs to his waiting bedroom.

LARRY LAY AWAKE IN THE DIM light from the moon that filtered through his sheer curtains, while Crystal's chest slowly rose and fell beneath the cream-colored sheet. The strange thing was, it seemed perfectly natural to have her here. He wasn't sure if it was the redecorating, the amount of time that had passed or simply his feelings for Crystal. But he could keep her here, in his room, in his bed, forever.

He placed a gentle kiss on her smooth, bare shoulder.

It was four-thirty. He'd usually be up and showered by now, but he didn't want to risk disturbing her. Regular people needed eight hours' sleep. Which was an advantage to him on some days, and a disadvantage on others. Today, he didn't want to wait three more hours to talk to Crystal.

He supposed a man took the good with the bad. His sleep cycle had enabled him to earn his PhD and teach full-time at the university, with the occasional consulting job for NASA, while managing the math department so perfectly that it kept the president of the university more than happy. Still, he wished he could just stay and gaze into Crystal's jade-green eyes.

As if reading his mind, she blinked them open.

"Hey," she yawned, her ruby lips curving into a smile.

"Hey, yourself." He brushed a lock of hair from her cheek.

"What time is it?"

"Four-thirty."

"You should be asleep."

"So should you."

She extracted her arm from beneath the sheet and ran her fingers over his beard-roughened chin. "I was."

"Did I wake you?"

"I don't think so. I was dreaming about apartment hunting."

"That doesn't sound good."

"It wasn't. But I have to do it."

"Today?" He supposed with her parents' impending move, she didn't dare waste any time.

She nodded, eyes fluttering closed. "I should have an early breakfast."

"What time is early for you?"

"Seven-thirty."

"I'll make breakfast."

She smiled.

"What do you like?" he asked.

"Anything." Her expression relaxed. "Anything," she whispered, and her breathing went even.

"Anything at seven-thirty," he mumbled. Then he kissed her on the forehead and slipped out of the bed.

He pulled on a pair of gym shorts and a clean T-shirt, then trotted down the stairs where Rufus met him. The pool didn't open until six, and he really needed to clear his head.

"What about it, buddy?" he asked the dog. "You up for a jog?"

Rufus wagged his tail and followed at Larry's heels into the kitchen. After a quick cup of coffee for him and a bowl of kibbles for Rufus, Larry donned his runners. They locked the front door and headed out to the street. It was still dark, but a faint blue glow had appeared on the eastern horizon, masking the stars.

They jogged down a deserted Versluce Street and onto the Bridge, then they headed into the park to do a lap around the pond on the bark-mulch trail. Rufus settled into the pace and seemed happy to stay at Larry's heels. Larry enjoyed the company, even if the dog did scare the mallard ducks paddling in the reeds near the shore.

When they made the wide turn at the end of the pond, the sun was peeking up over the hills. Larry's thoughts turned from gamma ray burst astrometry to the image of Crystal sleeping in his bed. Despite his vehement denial to Steve, Larry had thought a lot about the midlife crisis angle.

Was there some hormonal or genetic programming that attracted him to younger women at this stage? He hadn't ever noticed it before. He'd certainly met his share of twenty and thirty-something women in the past year, and he hadn't felt a spark with any of them, not a single flare or glow of desire.

This was all Crystal, plain and simple. And though he knew he should care about the age difference, he was falling too hard for her. And he couldn't bring himself to stop.

He found himself picking up the pace. He glanced at his watch. It was six-thirty, and he wanted to get home in time to make her something special for breakfast. Maybe waffles. Nice, crispy Belgian waffles with berries and whipped cream.

He'd have to stop at the store for whipping cream, but that was fine. There was a mini market on Waverly. It was only a small detour.

They'd sit out on his back deck, sipping coffee and watching the dew burn off the ferns and flowers in his garden. Larry smiled to himself, while Rufus barked at another flock of ducks.

They rose into the air, wings beating, the water rippling behind them. The day suddenly seemed full of promise. Larry's life seemed full of promise.

As soon as breakfast was over, he'd start planning their weekend in Pocono. Now that they were officially dating, he figured he could spend as much money on her as he liked.

"YOU'RE JOKING," SAID CRYSTAL, staring at the Web page of an ultra-luxury hotel suite in Pocono with a castle-like exterior. The suite had high ceilings, massive windows, a polished-wood chandelier, a corner fireplace, along with deep-cushioned couches, all complimented by a giant whirlpool tub and a canopied bed.

"You don't like it?" asked Larry, turning the laptop back toward him on the breakfast table out on his deck.

"I think it'll cost a fortune," said Crystal. She was sure there were several lovely family motels near the track.

"So what?" he asked.

"So are you made of money?"

"I'm a mathematician."

What the heck was that supposed to mean?

"And you said I could spend money on you once we were dating."

"I didn't mean you should take out a second mortgage."

He grinned. "I don't have a first mortgage."

"Neither do I." Crystal stretched her arms over her head.

She was wearing one of Larry's white dress shirts. It slipped up her thighs, and the cool morning air flowed over her skin. "Which reminds me. I have to get out there and apartment-hunt."

She polished off the remainder of her coffee. "Thanks for breakfast."

"You want some help?" he asked.

"I'm sure you have better things to do. Maybe some research to finish?" The last thing Crystal wanted was to become the visitor from hell. There was nothing worse than a sleepover guest who didn't know when the night was over. She needed to give Larry space.

"That's the thing about astrophysics research," he said.

She waited.

"I can't solve all the mysteries of the universe, I'll die long before my work is ever finished."

She leaned forward. "Then you better get started."

He grinned. "I got started when I was fifteen years old. And I'm really not all that much closer to any answers."

"Well, there's the ion propulsion engine thingee."

"Thingee?"

She nodded. "I believe that's the technical term."

"We're still working out the bugs on that. Aiming for 2010, actually. I think I can afford to take a day off."

"And you want to spend it looking at low-rent apartments in Charlotte?"

His eyes went flirty as he stared into hers. "Yeah."

"You're crazy."

He finished his own coffee, rising to his feet. "Statistically speaking, genius and insanity are very closely linked."

She stood with him. "Good to know."

"You want me to drive?"

Crystal really wasn't thrilled with the idea of taking Larry along. The kinds of apartments she could afford were going to be depressing and embarrassing. She was thinking about a one-bedroom basement, or maybe a third-floor walkup bachelor—something to keep expenses down while she looked for a new job.

"I don't want to take you away from anything important," she tried.

His expression sobered. "If you don't want me to come."

"It's not that," she lied.

His lips thinned and his eyes turned guarded. "I guess I misinterpreted—"

"Oh, hell," she spat out. Beating around the bush was getting her into even more trouble. "It's not you, okay? It's that I'm not going to be able to afford anything nice."

He looked relieved. "Then we'll find you something ugly."

She headed inside the house, muttering under her breath. "While you book the Emperor Suite at the Castle on the Hill."

"You might as well see how the other half lives," he told her easily, following behind. "Maybe it'll inspire you to work harder."

"I'm a writer," she countered. "We're supposed to be starving in some damp, little garret in Paris."

"Is that what we're looking for?" he asked. "A garret? I don't know if we have any garrets in Charlotte."

BY THREE O'CLOCK, THEY HADN'T found a damp garret or anything else that was suitable. Crystal didn't mind small, and she didn't mind worn; she did mind dirty, and she couldn't tolerate dangerous. It was also tough to find any place that would take Rufus.

"Had enough?" asked Larry as he slammed the driver's door and wrapped his hands around the steering wheel, staring in disgust at the plain, cinderblock building with bars on the ground-floor windows and graffiti across the service entrance.

Crystal clenched her fists around her hair, shaking her head and making a sound of disgust deep in her throat. "I just want something plain and simple and clean. Is that too much to ask?"

He turned to look at her, expression serious. "You might have to think about using Simon's money."

She immediately shook her head.

"You'd starve on the streets over a principle?"

"I'm not going to starve in the streets." She was going to find an apartment and a job, and she was going to live like a normal person.

"You can always rent a room from me."

"No, I can't."

"It'd be cheap."

She shot him a stare. "You know I can't do that."

He gave a nod to the group of teenage boys lounging on the front steps of the building. "Well, you can't stay here."

She didn't disagree with that. But there was a lot of real estate between social housing and Larry's place. "We don't even know where our relationship is going," she elaborated.

His grip tightened, so did his voice. "You're right. We don't."

She'd offended him, now. She never should have brought him along. "Can you take me back to my car?"

He turned his head. "You're giving up?"

"There's something else I want to do this afternoon."

He waited, but didn't ask for an explanation.

"It's for the kids," she admitted.

He waited some more, silently, patiently, while she remembered she could trust him and count on him. He'd proved as much the night at Myrtle Pond.

"Sunday night was unsettling," she told him. "Amber's drinking too much, and she's got stars in her eyes over Zane. She might even tell him about the money. I want to pick up a cell phone for Jennifer. You know, program my number into it, just in case."

"Auntie Crystal, on call, day or night?"

"Something like that."

Larry reached for the ignition. "It's a good idea. Can we pick up the kids?"

"Why?"

"You'll want to show her how to use it, charge it. She might even want to pick it out. If it's a cool phone, she's more likely to keep it with her."

Crystal nodded. That was definitely a good idea. "How do you think of these things?"

Larry smiled. "I raised a son, remember?"

Of course he had. She'd never been introduced to Steve, but she knew him by reputation. By all accounts, he was a fine man.

She dialed her sister and caught her on a coffee break.

"Are the kids going to day care after school today?" she asked Amber.

"Of course," said Amber, her tone telling Crystal she was still upset about the night before.

Crystal tried not to sigh in frustration. "I was thinking about picking them up and, I don't know, maybe going out for ice cream or doing a little shopping."

"You are?" Amber's voice perked up. "Would you mind keeping them for dinner?"

A date with Zane, no doubt.

"I don't mind at all," said Crystal. "What time do you want me to drop them off tonight?"

"Can I call you later?"

"Sure." Good thing the kids had spare pajamas at Crystal's place.

"Thanks, Crystal. You're the best."

Yeah, yeah. She was the best for the next twelve hours anyway.

"Talk to you tonight then. Don't forget to call the day care."

"I won't. Bye."

"Bye." Crystal pushed the off button. "I'm keeping them over dinner."

Larry flipped on his turn signal and turned onto the main road. "Zane again?"

"I'm sure." She slipped the phone back into her purse. "The day care's on Governor Road, just past the plaza." She stared out the window for a minute, letting the stately oaks flash by her vision. "I can't decide if I'm being a good aunt or simply being an enabler."

"You're being a good aunt."

She turned back to Larry. "You're biased."

"Because I'm sleeping with you?"

"Exactly."

"Think about it," he said. "Would Amber stop seeing Zane if you weren't babysitting?"

"No," Crystal admitted.

"There you go. There's nothing you can do to alter her behavior. From what you've said, there's a pattern to these reunions, and you simply have to let it run its course."

"And keep the fallout from hurting the kids."

"That's right. And that's exactly what you're doing." He reached across the seat to cover her hand with his. "You're a good aunt, Crystal. And you're a good person."

His sweet intentions warmed her heart.

"You're still biased," she reminded him.

"You forget. I'm a scientist. We're trained to be impartial."

"I remember. You're a man. You're anthropologically selected to think with your hormones."

His gaze warmed. "I'm thinking with them now."

So was she. "See what I mean?"

He nodded toward two blocks up the busy street. "That the parking lot?"

"Take a left at the light, and you can pull right in."

Larry stopped his car in the pickup lane while Crystal jumped out. She spoke to the entry attendant, who confirmed that Amber had given her permission for Crystal to take the kids.

The kids were thrilled to see her, doubly thrilled when they learned Larry was along as well.

"I'm going to be a fighter jet pilot," David called, swinging his backpack into Larry's compact backseat and clambering in.

"It's a tough job. The F-15 Eagle, for example, has a top speed of Mach 2.5," said Larry. "That's 1694 miles an hour at thirty thousand feet. A whopping 1902 miles an hour at sea level."

"Whoa!"

"You sure you want to go that fast?"

"Yes!" David shouted, with a bounce on the seat.

Jennifer paused before getting in the car, looking up at Crystal. "Is Mommy okay?" she asked in a quiet voice.

An ache flashing across her chest, Crystal smoothed Jennifer's hair back from her forehead and forced out a cheery smile. "Of course, she's okay. She's at work right now, but she said you could come to my place for dinner if you wanted."

Jennifer smiled and her narrow shoulders seemed to relax. Crystal realized she needed to have another talk with Amber. It looked like waiting out Zane might be too hard on Jennifer.

"Fighter pilots always wear their safety harness," said Larry, and David immediately searched for the two ends of his seat belt.

"They wear helmets, too," said David as he buckled in.

"Safety equipment is very important," said Larry, gazing expectantly at Crystal.

"Oops." She grabbed her own seat belt.

He smiled. "Fighter pilots have really cool flight suits."

"And parachutes," chimed David.

"That's right," said Larry as they pulled out of the day care's pickup lane and back into traffic. "Do you know what happens if a fighter pilot pulls the ejection lever?"

David's voice was hushed. "What?"

Crystal found herself paying attention along with Jennifer.

"The aircraft canopy comes off, an explosive charge goes off under his seat, and he and his chair are propelled at twelve g's into the air where a parachute deploys, sending them safely back to earth."

"And then the plane blows up," said David.

"It definitely crashes," Larry agreed.

"What if there are people underneath?" asked Jennifer, her forehead furrowing.

Larry cast a worried glance into the rearview mirror. "There usually aren't," he said in a cheerful voice. "A very small percentage of the earth's surface is populated. Add up all the deserts and jungles and farmland. Did you know that seventy-one percent of the world is covered in water?"

Jennifer went from worried to impressed. "Do you know everything, Uncle Larry?" she asked.

Crystal's and Larry's eyes met over the honorary title. She wasn't touching it with a ten-foot pole.

"I know a lot of things," he told Jennifer. "Mostly scientific things."

"Arithmetic," said David with a scowl.

"Arithmetic is important," said Larry. "You can't be a pilot without learning arithmetic."

"I guess," said David, drumming his feet against the back of Larry's seat.

"Anybody up for South Park Mall?" asked Larry.

"Milkshakes," sang David.

Jennifer sat straight up, looking to Crystal. "Can we?"

AT THE ELECTRONICS STORE, Larry urged David toward the toy section, leaving Crystal alone with Jennifer.

"Do any of your friends have cell phones?" Crystal asked, as they slowed beside the display case.

"Melinda Bergman has the AS-207, so she can take pictures. And Alicia Wong has a Blingbot. But her parents are rich."

"Have you ever thought you might like one?"

Jennifer looked at her curiously. They both knew Amber wasn't into extravagant gifts, and Grandma thought a land line worked perfectly fine, thank you very much.

"I was thinking," said Crystal, lifting a slim, pearlescent pink model. "That having one might be handy."

"Mom would just say no," Jennifer sighed, her attention going to the shiny black one at the far end.

Good taste, that girl. It was top of the line.

"It would be very practical," Crystal continued. "Like, I could call you. And you could call me. It wouldn't matter where you were, or what you were doing."

Jennifer looked at her, a light obviously going on in her brain. "Like when Mom was late or something."

"Yeah," Crystal admitted. "If Mom was ever late."

Jennifer chewed her bottom lip.

"You could call your friends," said Crystal.

"It's not my birthday."

"No, it's not."

"And it's not Christmas, or even Easter."

"Mayday?" Crystal tried.

"It's June," said Jennifer.

"Special Secret Surprise Present Day?"

Jennifer giggled.

"I just decided when that should be," said Crystal. "Right now."

Jennifer looked at the phones and sobered.

Crystal crouched down so that they were eye level. "We both know your dad can be unpredictable."

The young girl nodded.

"So, just in case. Just for emergencies, like when you practice fire drills at school. Mostly you'll be calling your friends at recess. But we can put my phone number on a speed dial button. And you can call me. Anytime."

"Like, if David has a bad dream. And Mommy won't wake up?"

"Sure," said Crystal, forced to blink back tears for a second.

Jennifer nodded. "David might need you."

"He might," said Crystal. "And he's too young to take care of a phone."

Jennifer nodded again.

"So, does it seem like a good idea to you?"

"Melinda Bergman would sure be surprised."

"She will," Crystal agreed with a smile, just as Larry and David appeared.

"So, tell me," said Larry. "Which is the coolest phone here?"

Jennifer's shoulders squared, and her chest puffed out ever so slightly. She pointed to the slim black phone with the touch screen.

"Excellent taste," said Larry, lifting it up.

Crystal silently and sarcastically thanked him very much on behalf of her credit card provider. It was going to take her a few months to pay the darn thing off. Still, if it meant Jennifer would keep it charged and with her, it was worth it. You couldn't put a price on safety.

"The LG-Quantum it is," said Larry, flagging down a sales clerk.

Before Crystal knew what was happening, Larry had handed over his credit card.

"Oh, no, you don't," she muttered to him, following one clerk toward the cash register, while another walked Jennifer to a demonstration counter to go over the phone instructions.

"You said I could," Larry countered, putting an arm around her shoulders to slow her down.

"I did not."

"You said I couldn't spend money on you unless we were dating."

"That's ridicu—"

"Well, we're dating now." His voice went lower. "By any benchmark, we are totally dating."

"I never said you could spend money on my niece."

"The phone's not for your niece. It's for you. To give you piece of mind."

"That's the lamest, most convoluted—"

"Most logical argument you've ever heard." He talked right overtop of her.

"Would you care for one of our prepaid plans?" asked the clerk.

"Yes," said Larry.

"No," said Crystal.

"There's a fifteen percent discount on plans over twelve months."

"Sounds good," said Larry.

Crystal gritted her teeth. "I'm paying you back."

"Yeah?"

"Yeah."

"Well, good luck with that."

"You are impossible."

He nodded toward the kids. "Look."

Jennifer stood with rapt attention, watching the phone demonstration. The clerk handed her the phone, letting her try something. Another phone, somewhere in the store, rang, and she grinned.

Then her phone made a chiming noise, followed by a screeching rock song.

"Pick that one," said David.

Jennifer shook her head, while the ring switched to symphony music.

"Your card, sir," said the sales clerk, and Crystal admitted defeat.

Jennifer had her phone. That was the important thing. And Crystal would figure out how to pay Larry back somehow.

CHAPTER ELEVEN

AFTER THEY PURCHASED THE phone, Larry wanted to make sure that David didn't feel left out. So he'd offered everybody a ride in his airplane.

Crystal graciously wedged into the backseat with Jennifer, and David spent the entire hour in the copilot's seat with his nose pressed up against the glass.

Afterward, they stopped for burgers at a fast food restaurant. It was nearly bedtime when they stumbled laughing up the stairs to Crystal's apartment.

"Can Rufus sleep on my bed again?" David called as they piled through the doorway.

Feeling unaccountably good, Larry draped his arm loosely around Crystal's shoulders. Then he stopped short at the sight of Crystal's mother standing in the kitchen.

She took in Crystal and the kids, and then her gaze stopped on Larry.

"Larry Grosso," she confirmed, her expression not nearly as welcoming as it had been the last time they talked.

"Stella," he responded with a nod, guiltily removing his arm.

"Grandma, Grandma," David cried, breaking from the pack. "Uncle Larry took us for a ride in his airplane."

All three adults froze on "uncle."

"It was awesome," said David.

"Hi, Mom," Crystal quickly put in, moving forward.

"I see you have the kids," said Stella.

"They're staying over," Crystal explained.

Larry gestured behind him to the door. "I guess, maybe I'd better—"

"Nonsense," said Stella, eyes glittering. "Since you seem to be part of the family."

Larry looked to Crystal, and she sent him a clear "it's now or never" look back.

"I'll put the kids to bed," Crystal said, ushering the children toward the spare bedroom and closing the door behind them.

In mere seconds, Larry was alone with Stella, and the silence boomed hollowly around them.

She folded her arms over her chest. "I didn't realize you were dating my daughter."

Well, that certainly cured the silence problem.

"We started off as friends," Larry said honestly.

"*Uncle* Larry."

"I don't think David knew what to call me." He thought about offering Stella coffee or tea, but realized she was more the hostess than he. Pretending otherwise might offend her.

"I know your brother," said Stella.

Larry nodded his acknowledgement.

"And I know your nephew." She paused. "And I know you're a lot older than my daughter."

Larry moved toward the living room, uncomfortably hovering in the entryway. "I realize that, too," he said.

"And what are your intentions?"

"I have no intentions." Right now his only intention was to spend as much time as humanly possible with Crystal. He hadn't allowed himself to look beyond that.

"She wants children," said Stella.

"I think we're getting ahead of ourselves."

"So, you're only interested in a fling. Is that it?"

"No." He realized the word had been sharp and forced himself to tone his voice down. "No. I'm not only interested in a fling. I like your daughter very much."

Stella harrumphed her skepticism.

Larry glanced toward the bedroom door, willing Crystal to join them again.

"Stella."

"You like my daughter?"

"Yes, I do."

"You want to do right by her?"

"Of course."

"Then don't encourage her in this."

Larry took offense. This relationship was hardly one-sided, and Crystal was perfectly capable of making up her own mind. "I don't think you understand."

"I understand perfectly," said Stella. "You are not good for my daughter. Oh, she might be bowled over by your family and—"

"Wait just a minute." Larry had hardly used his famous family to entice Crystal into his life. Crystal, quite frankly, wasn't the slightest bit in awe of his family.

"No, *you* wait a minute," said Stella, gesturing at the center of his chest with her index finger. "Crystal is my daughter. She's already had her heart broken when Simon died. She doesn't need that to happen again. Her life is just starting. You are nearly ready to retire."

Larry drew back at that. "I am nowhere near ready to retire."

The bedroom door opened. "Wash your face and brush your teeth," Crystal called as the kids trotted down the hall.

Smiling, she looked at Larry, then to her mother, then back to Larry. Her smile disappeared. "What?"

He glanced to the open bathroom door and gave his head a slight shake.

The three stood in silence for a moment, then David raced down the hall, arms out, making airplane engine noises. "Come on, Rufus," he called to the dog. "We're going in for a landing." He flung himself onto the bed.

"Come on, boy," Crystal called to Rufus as a flannel-clad Jennifer made her way more slowly down the hall and into the bedroom.

Kids settled, Crystal reappeared, clicking the door shut behind her. "Something wrong?"

"I was saying—" Larry began, but was cut off.

"You're too smart to be getting yourself into something like this," snapped Stella.

"Mom, we're not—"

"Where can it possibly lead?"

Crystal moved into the living room. "You're embarrassing me, Mom."

"What's embarrassing is you taking up with a man twice your age."

"He's not twice my age."

But Larry had already done the math. It wasn't that far off. He and Crystal were ready to accept the difference, but if Stella and Steve's reactions were anything to go by, how well was the rest of the world likely to react?

Larry didn't care for himself, but Crystal shouldn't have to put up with it. And there was the question of children. Even if he did want to start over, which he didn't, he'd had a vasectomy. After Steve was born, the doctors told Libby that her high blood pressure might make it dangerous for her to have more children. Larry had made sure there was no risk to Elizabeth's health on that front.

"Mother," said Crystal. "Larry and I have had exactly three dates."

He made it four, but wasn't about to quibble.

"So now *you're* saying it's just a fling."

"I'm saying it's a date."

"Four dates," said Larry, earning a glare from Crystal.

"It's too soon for you or anybody else to press the panic button," she said.

"What about children?"

Crystal held up her hands. "Stop. I know you want more grandchildren."

"This isn't about me."

Crystal started to laugh. "Then who is it about?"

Stella looked affronted. "You, of course."

"Good. Then we can stop talking. Because I'm perfectly fine with dating Larry."

Stella opened her mouth, but she seemed to have temporarily run out of arguments.

"Was there a reason you're here, Mom?"

Stella blinked. "Kenny Carmichael."

Larry knew Kenny was the major player in the Softco purchase.

Crystal sighed. "He wants to let me go."

Stella gave her head a little shake. "There you go. Jumping to conclusions. Just like you always do." She looked to Larry. "You see why I worry about this girl?"

Under no circumstances was he taking a piece of that.

"Kenny wants you to work more hours." She glanced around. "And you can stay in the apartment, of course."

"I can?" Crystal asked in a small voice.

"It's in the sales agreement."

"That's very generous."

Stella nodded. "We're your parents. We want what's best for you." She gave Larry a pointed look.

He wanted what was best for Crystal, too. But he didn't know how to convince Stella that was true.

"Good night, Mom." Crystal moved forward to give her mother a kiss on the cheek.

Stella didn't look happy, but most of her anger seemed to have abated. With a warning glance in Larry's direction, she headed for the door.

When it shut behind her, he breathed a sigh of relief.

"Sorry about that," said Crystal.

"Nothing for you to be sorry about."

"She's always been, well, a straight shooter." Crystal flopped down on the couch. "She's never put much stock in emotion. You know, I think she'd have gone with arranged marriages if she'd had her way. The man's job, his family connections, family history of diseases and longevity."

Larry eased down next to her on the soft sofa. "You know, my son reacted in much the same way the other day."

Crystal twisted her head. "Steve doesn't want you to date me?"

"He thinks I'm having a midlife crisis."

She was silent for a few heartbeats. "Are you?"

He reached up, smoothed back her hair and smiled. "You mean am I going to come to my senses one day soon and realize you're not good enough for me?"

"Something like that."

"Never happen." He paused. "You on the other hand, could easily, and quite rightfully, come to your senses."

She shook her head, taking his hand in hers. "Never happen," she whispered.

"It's way too soon to know that."

"No, it's not." She kissed his hand and rubbed it up against her cheek. "I'm falling in love with you, Larry."

"Not the greatest idea," he warned.

"*That's* what you have to say back?"

"No." He turned to fully face her. "What I have to say back, is that I'm already in love with you. But that doesn't mean our detractors are wrong."

"They don't understand," said Crystal.

"On the contrary. They understand perfectly. They just don't happen to think we're a good idea."

"Good thing they don't get a vote."

"They're our families." And they've made some perfectly valid points. "You want children."

"Someday," she agreed.

"I can't have children."

He could see the surprise in her eyes. "You have Steve. Men can—"

"I had surgery," he explained.

"Oh."

He tried to gauge how the revelation had affected her. "Nothing about this is simple."

She put on a brave smile. "It's simple at the moment. We're not going to do what my mother did. People don't go on three dates—"

"Four."

"—and decide their entire future. We're going to Pocono. We're going to have a great time together. And we're not going to worry about anything else."

Larry hesitated. She was right. People didn't have to decide their future up front. But he also knew that the more time that went by, the greater the risk one of them would get hurt.

He could handle it, if it was just him. He couldn't handle it, if it was Crystal who paid the emotional price.

"Things can change," she continued. "Look at my employment and my apartment situation."

Larry couldn't help but smile. "Wasn't that a waste of a day?"

"We learned a lot about the seamy side of Charlotte."

"Sweetheart, those were things I didn't really want to learn."

"Pocono," she repeated. "I'll even stay in that fancy-ass castle suite with you," she cajoled.

"You will?"

She nodded.

He sighed. What was he going to do, cancel the weekend? Not much chance of that.

"You going to work tomorrow?" he asked.

She nodded. "Better talk to Kenny and make myself some money. You?"

"I have to head up to Myrtle Pond and work on the house." He'd been putting it off all week. "Pick you up on Friday?"

She nodded, as he started to rise.

"You don't have to leave," she pointed out.

Oh yes, he did. "The kids are in the next room, and I have this sneaking feeling your mother's waiting to see my taillights exit the parking lot."

Crystal gave in graciously, and he headed home, telling himself Stella, Steve and Dean were all wrong, and that Crystal might change her mind about children.

The scientist in him knew he was grasping at straws. But the mathematician in him understood chaos theory. Despite all the complications, he couldn't completely discount the notion that he and Crystal might have been preordained.

AFTER DROPPING THE KIDS off for the second-last day of school, Crystal spent the morning alternating between working on her cookbook and daydreaming about Larry.

He couldn't have children.

What did that mean?

Did it mean anything at all? They'd barely started dating. It was way too early to be thinking about a white dress, a dog and a picket fence.

As if he read her mind, Rufus rose from where he was sleeping on the mat and padded over to the sofa. He nudged her laptop a few inches and rested his head on her knee, squinting his eyes against the breeze that wafted in through the open window.

"Okay, so we've got the dog part already," she told him, scratching between his ears, trying not to feel maudlin at the choice between Larry and children.

For goodness sake, she didn't even know if the choice was hers to make yet. Their feelings were deep, but it was the first blush of romance. And Larry was clearly having second thoughts, after her mother and his son had expressed their opinions.

Rufus gave a heartfelt sigh that seemed to echo her own emotions.

He'd spent the night sleeping on the foot of David's bed, and David hadn't made a peep. The dog had clearly bonded with David. As he had with Larry. Crystal smiled. He'd even started spending more time with her. Memories of his original owner must be fading.

She leaned down and cupped his head with her hands, stroking the damaged ear. "We're going to be okay, you and me," she promised.

His brown eyes gazed up at her with trust and adoration.

There was a knock on the door, and Rufus immediately

went on alert. He didn't bark, but he trotted into the kitchen, positioning himself at the end of the hall, watchful while Crystal moved to the door.

Through the sheers on the window, she could see a strange man on the porch. The man didn't look particularly dangerous. He was about sixty-five, wore a neat business suit and was carrying a briefcase. Still, she was glad of the dog's presence.

She twisted the lock and opened the door, wondering if he was selling something. Her little apartment tucked behind and atop of the Softco complex didn't normally attract salespeople. But you never knew.

"Ms. Crystal Hayes?" the man asked.

"Yes?" Her curiosity grew.

"I'm Fred Smythe, attorney for Mr. William Chandler."

The name meant nothing to her, and for a second she wondered if it was a scam of some kind. She leaned against the end of the door, her skepticism rising.

"Can I help you with something?"

"I tried to call but I seem to have the wrong phone number." He glanced around. "Would it be possible to come inside and talk?"

"I don't think so." She felt Rufus's body against the back of her knee and wondered if her body language had brought him closer. Smart dog.

Fred Smythe cleared his throat and straightened his tie. "In that case." He paused. "I'll get right to… Mr. Chandler was involved in an automobile accident on May twenty-second."

Were they looking for a witness? "I didn't see—"

"He was, unfortunately, killed in the accident." The man's gaze strayed to Rufus. "I understand you may have been caring for his dog?"

Crystal's stomach hollowed out, and her shoulders slumped. They'd come for Rufus?

No. She couldn't let them.

"May we talk inside?" Fred asked again.

"Of course," she choked out, stepping back to let the man in.

She gestured to her small kitchen table. "Please."

Fred glanced around before taking a seat on the small, wooden chair, laying his briefcase on the table.

Crystal sat across from him, while Rufus took a position at her feet. She swallowed, folding her hands on the tabletop. "Do they want him back?" she rasped. "The family?"

Fred flipped open the clasps on his briefcase. "Mr. Chandler didn't have family."

Hope rose within Crystal.

"I was left with the task of finding the right home for Aldo."

Rufus perked up at the sound of his name.

Crystal looked down at Rufus. "Aldo?" she asked him.

He cocked his head and blinked at her, seeming to confirm she'd finally got it right.

She patted him on the head. "Aldo," she repeated. "Never would have guessed that one." Then she turned her attention back to Fred.

"You were a difficult woman to find," said Fred.

"I found him tied up to a tree," she explained. "I left my name at the Treatsy-Sweetsy."

"It took them a while to remember you had. And the scrunched napkin was difficult to read."

Crystal thought back to the young clerk. She could see how the napkin might have gotten lost. "I guess I should have called back again."

She glanced back down at Rufus, Aldo. Maybe, subconsciously, she hadn't wanted to be found. She certainly knew that she didn't want to give him up now, for David's sake if nothing else.

"I have this nephew," she told Fred, "he and Rufus have really bonded. And, well, Rufus and I…" She scratched between his ears. "It took us a little while longer, but we're pretty cool now, too. Is there, like, an application form or something I could fill out to try to keep him?" She just hoped it didn't involve a credit check.

If money was an issue, maybe she could get Larry to apply. They could have joint custody or something. And Larry had a backyard. He might be an all-around better candidate.

"You want to keep the dog?" asked Fred.

She gave a quick nod. "Absolutely. He's a wonderful dog."

Fred glanced at Rufus, took in the food and water dishes and the leash hanging on the coat hook in the hallway.

"You've spent some money on him?"

"A little bit," she answered. "Just the essentials so far. We did rent a crate to fly him to Dover."

"You took the dog to Dover?"

Crystal smiled as she remembered the trip. "He loved the seashore. Didn't quite know what to do with the salt water, but he played fetch forever." She brought herself back to the present. "I know I'm in an apartment, but there's a wonderful park right behind us, with a pond. Rufus loves to walk, and he plays with my nephew when he comes over. He even sleeps at the foot of David's bed."

"David?"

"My nephew. He and my niece sleep over sometimes."

It seemed to Crystal that kids involved in Rufus's life would be a good thing.

"And you're not looking for any money to care for the dog?"

Crystal drew back, startled. "Money from who?"

"From Mr. Chandler's estate."

"No. Of course not. I never even met Mr. Chandler." Then she had a thought. She leaned forward. "Would you like me to buy Rufus?"

Since Larry had sprung for the cell phone, Crystal could come up with *some* money for the dog. Not a lot. But then Rufus didn't seem like a show animal or anything.

A smile grew on Fred's face. "There's no need to buy Aldo. Mr. Chandler's express wishes were that I find a loving home for his best friend. I believe I've found that in you."

Crystal's chest tightened, and she was forced to blink back a couple of ridiculous tears. "Thank you," she told him, stretching forward to clasp his hands in hers.

Fred shook his head, looking uncomfortable. "No need to thank me. It's my job."

"Thank you all the same." She reached down to pat Rufus, or Aldo, or whoever he wanted to be.

Fred opened his briefcase and slipped on a pair of reading glasses. "There is a small matter of money."

She nodded. "Okay." Maybe there was a fee or something. No problem. She got to keep Rufus. That was all that mattered.

"Mr. Chandler left provisions for Rufus's care and feeding."

Crystal didn't understand.

"In fact," said Fred. "The bulk of his estate was set aside for that purpose."

"You're giving *me* money?"

"Yes." He pulled out a sheaf of papers. "Five million, six hundred and thirty-two thousand dollars."

She stared at him, trying to turn his words into something that made sense inside her head.

"Aside from a few bequests to charitable and service organizations, Mr. Chandler left his estate to his dog. Or, rather, to the new owner of his dog."

"That's insane," said Crystal. "I can't take that money. Dog food is maybe twenty bucks a week."

Fred gave her a wide smile. "Nevertheless, this will is a legal contract. You want the dog, you get the money."

It was a ridiculous amount of money. "Why didn't you keep him?"

Fred peered over the top of his glasses. "My task was to find him a good home, not to keep him. Besides, it would have been a blatant conflict of interest."

Crystal subconsciously pulled back. "It's a conflict of interest for me, too."

"No, it's not."

The thought of that much money simply made her panic. She couldn't spend it on herself. It would be wrong. And she'd never manage to spend it all on Rufus. Even if they chartered him his own plane to NASCAR races, she'd never spend it all. They'd have to rent him doggie VIP suites, with all you can eat goose-liver pâté.

Which would be ridiculous.

"You said something about charities?" she tried. "Could I donate the money to Mr. Chandler's favorite charities?"

Fred nodded. "You could. But you might want to consider setting up something in his name. A charitable foundation for abandoned pets, for example."

What a great idea. "Could you help me do that?"

He closed his briefcase and replaced the glasses in his

pocket. "I'd be very pleased to help you. But I want you to give this some thought. And remember, there's nothing wrong in spending some or all of the money on yourself."

Crystal shook her head.

"Mr. Chandler's only wish was that Aldo have a loving home." He glanced at the dog. "I'm delighted to know I've been able to arrange that." He rose from his chair and handed her a business card. "I'll be in touch."

"Thank you," she said, numbly staring down at his name. Then she rose and looked up at him. "Thank you for Rufus."

She couldn't wrap her head around the five million dollars. And she didn't have to. She'd let Fred take care of the details of a charitable trust. All she needed was enough money for dog food.

CHAPTER TWELVE

LARRY KNEW HE NEEDED TO GIVE Crystal some space. The question of whether to continue the relationship was easy from his side. She was a beautiful woman who made him happy, and he loved her.

From her side, it was considerably more complicated. Though he wasn't anywhere near retirement at the moment, he'd certainly get there before she would. And he couldn't give her children. Even if by some miracle of modern science, he could reverse the surgery, he wouldn't. It wouldn't be fair to become a new father at this stage. While he could still play catch, and do any other children's physical activity, the same might not hold true in ten years.

"You look tense," said Nash, handing Larry a cold can of beer as the sun set on Nash's deck overlooking Myrtle Pond.

"I'm fine," said Larry. He didn't particularly want to get into a heart-to-heart with Nash.

They'd been working on the Victorian all day, and he'd been able to put everything else out of his mind. But now that work was stopped, he couldn't help wondering about Crystal. Had she finished work for the day? Did she have the kids? Was Zane making a nuisance of himself? And how was Rufus?

Nash took a seat in one of the padded deck chairs, and Larry followed suit.

"I asked around about that Zane Crandell," said Nash, crossing an ankle over the opposite knee.

Larry didn't understand. "Asked around to whom?"

Nash shrugged, taking a sip of the beer. "Just some guys I know. He's got a couple of assaults on his file in Atlanta."

"You know Atlanta cops?"

Nash nodded. "Some. They were bar fights, nothing domestic. But the man doesn't drink well."

"I'd be surprised to learn he does anything well," Larry put in. Zane had struck him as a loser with a capital *L*.

"Job as a night janitor. Low-rent apartment. A bit of a gambling issue, but nobody's looking to break his kneecaps or anything."

Larry gave a cold laugh. "Too bad."

"He touched the sister?" asked Nash.

"She says not."

"If he steps out of line, I can have somebody tune him up."

Larry squinted at Nash. "Who exactly do you know in Atlanta?"

A shrewdness came into Nash's eyes, something Larry didn't remember seeing before.

"Just some guys, who know some guys."

"I thought you said you were an architect."

If Nash wasn't an architect, he was the best fake Larry had ever met. He was an excellent builder, and facts and figures came out of his mouth in an almost encyclopedic manner. Larry recognized it, since he could do it himself.

Which gave him pause. Nash was one genius of an architect. And he'd chucked it all to run a bait shop?

"I am an architect," said Nash.

"For who? The mob?"

Nash grinned. "Right. I've been running their office tower development division on the Eastern Seaboard."

Okay, maybe not the mob. But there was something....

"Why'd you move to Myrtle Pond?" he tried.

Nash didn't answer, his expression inscrutable.

Larry felt a shiver run up his spine. He bought some time by taking a chug of his rapidly warming beer. "With my IQ, I guess I should be smart enough to know when to shut up and stop asking questions."

"Yeah. And especially as a researcher on the N-52 Isis project."

Larry froze. "*What* did you say?"

Nash gave him a look that said that Larry knew perfectly well what he'd said. He'd just tossed out the name of a top secret satellite project that, maybe, fifty guys in the world knew Larry was involved in.

"NSA?" asked Larry, his eyes squinting down at the waning light. "The military?"

"No initials you'd recognize."

"But, the good guys," Larry confirmed.

"The good guys," said Nash.

Then another unsettling thought hit Larry. "You're not here because of me, are you?"

Nash laughed, tipping back his head. "No offense, Larry. But you're nowhere near important enough for me to guard."

"Any danger to Myrtle Pond?"

Nash polished off his beer, stood up and hit the deck lights. "No one's going to find me here. Nobody's even looking."

Larry nodded, knowing that was as much information as he'd get, also knowing that was as much information as he wanted. If Nash knew Larry was working on the Isis project, he also knew Larry could be trusted; otherwise he wouldn't have revealed even that much.

Nash grabbed a couple more beers from the cooler. "So, if you need this Zane jerk tuned up, you just let me know."

Larry was sorely tempted. "Not the kind of solution I'm used to."

Nash set an unopened beer on the table next to Larry. "Likely not the kind of problem you're used to, either."

Larry couldn't disagree with that.

His mind snapped back to his other problem. "Let me ask you this." It was obvious he could trust Nash. "If you cared about a woman, but the circumstances were all wrong, would you walk away?"

"You're asking the wrong guy."

"Why's that?"

"Because the circumstances have never been right for me."

"So, what do you do?"

"You walk away from the ones you care about." Nash paused. "And sleep with the ones you don't."

"That's depressing."

"Isn't it though?"

Larry popped the tab on his second beer. "You and I are complete opposites." The last woman Larry had either cared about or slept with, he married.

"Which is why I can't see you being wrong for anybody," said Nash. "You're a freakin' Boy Scout."

"If I were a Boy Scout, I'd have walked away from her already." And that was the truth. It wasn't that Larry didn't know the right thing to do. He was simply too selfish to do it.

"Why?" Nash demanded.

"I'm too old."

"Horseshit."

"Eloquent argument."

"You don't have to be eloquent when you're right."

"She has her entire life ahead of her."

"From what I could see, she wants to spend part of it with you."

"And when I die?"

"Excuse me?"

"What happens to her when I die?"

Nash's voice rose with incredulity. "Well, hopefully, she gets a fat life insurance settlement and can grieve in the South Pacific."

Larry started to laugh. "You should practice what you preach, you know."

"How am I not?"

"If you're not afraid to leave a widow, then get into a relationship. Find a nice girl. Get married."

"Like a nice girl would marry me."

"Why not?"

Nash seemed to give it a moment's thought. "Because I'd have to lie to her every minute of every day."

Fair point. Larry supposed neither of them were particularly good husband material. He'd give Crystal some space, let her weigh the cons. Maybe she'd decide on her own to break things off. If she didn't? Then, at some point he'd have to be a man about it.

CRYSTAL GAZED AT LARRY'S profile in the first-class cabin of the 757. He'd seemed more than willing to oblige when she'd suggested they leave for Pocono on Saturday morning instead of Friday night. It meant they'd miss some of the pre-race activities at the track, but it also meant that Jennifer and David would be with their grand-mother the entire time Crystal was gone.

Crystal had had a long talk with Kenny about both her job and her apartment, so she was resting easy on those fronts. Though there did still remain the matter of William Chandler's bequest.

Given that he'd paid for first-class tickets, and the fact that Larry owned an airplane and two houses, she was guessing he was used to dealing with money. His family, at least, must have a pile of it to be so heavily involved in NASCAR. He seemed like a good person to approach with the problem.

She turned in her roomy seat, addressing him across their shared table of pre-flight champagne and orange juice.

"So," she began, trying to frame the situation into a couple of succinct sentences. "I've got this five million dollars."

He turned. "Excuse me?"

"Five million," she repeated with a nod of affirmation.

"And we were looking for an apartment on Roolan Street?"

"Well, I didn't have the money then."

"What? You knocked over a bank while I was away?"

"It's Rufus's money."

"Oh." Larry nodded. "Well, that explains it."

"Quit messing around."

He grinned. "Sorry. Tell me what you're talking about."

The flight attendant came by to remove their glasses as the plane lurched to a taxi, and the safety demonstration came on their screens.

Crystal gave Larry the rundown on the lawyer's visit.

"You sure this is legit?" he asked after she'd finished.

"If it's a scam, it's pretty elaborate."

"Did he ask you for any money?"

She gave Larry a look of disbelief. "I don't have any money. But no, he didn't ask for any money."

"Well, did he give you any money?"

"It's supposed to come next week."

"You have a lawyer?"

"No."

"You mind if I let mine look at the check and the paperwork?"

She waved his question away. "Whatever. What do you think I should do with the money? Do you like the idea of setting up a trust for homeless animals?"

"I think you should invest it."

"Why?"

"Then you can spend the interest and keep the principle into perpetuity. At eight percent, rock-solid investments, no risk, you'd have four hundred thousand a year. If you wanted to play around a little—"

"And I could take the four hundred thousand and run the trust."

"Or pay your rent."

"Dog food comes out of that money, Professor. Nothing else."

The jet engines whined as the aircraft gained speed on the runway. "I've never met a woman with more money and less inclination to spend it."

"It's not my money."

"It's all your money."

"I don't have a moral right to it."

"Neither does anyone else. And you have the signing authority."

She leaned back in her seat. "You're a mercenary man, Professor Grosso."

"Damn straight."

"Okay," she challenged, as the aircraft lifted smoothly from the runway, taking aim at a clear blue sky. "If it was your dog, your windfall, what would you do with it?"

That stopped him for a moment. "That's a completely different question."

"How is it different?"

"Because I don't need the money."

"You're telling me five million dollars doesn't have the power to completely change your life?"

He gave her a dead-on gaze.

"No way," she accused. He did not have that kind of money already. He was a college professor. His family's money?

"Ermanometry," he said. "Taken as a whole, the stock market is geometrically perfect."

This was too much. "You got rich through some secret mathematical formula."

"Basically."

"And you're telling me you don't need my measly five million dollars."

"Five million dollars isn't measly." A light came on behind his hazel eyes. "But I could double it for you."

"Is that illegal?"

He looked affronted. "Of course it's not illegal. Anybody who took the trouble to do the research could do exactly the same thing."

She gave a wry smile. "Or anybody who takes the trouble to sleep with the guy who did the research."

It took a second for the irreverent meaning to hit him. But then he grinned. "Now you're catching on."

She reached for his hand and twined their fingers together, tired of worrying about the money for the moment. "So, what are we doing in Pocono?"

"Checking into the hotel. After that, I'm open to suggestions." He raised her hand and kissed the back of her knuckles. "As long as it involves the whirlpool tub."

"I meant at the track. I assume we're ready to publicly own up to dating?"

Something flickered in his eyes, turning them golden for a split second before he blinked the emotion away. "We'll own up to dating."

"Good."

"You know there'll be some concerns. Steve has stated his position."

"Patsy's fine with it."

"Dean's not."

QUALIFYING WAS WELL UNDERWAY by the time Crystal and Larry made it to the track in the midafternoon. Hand in hand, they wound their way through the infield in the general direction of Dean and Patsy's motor home. Patsy had promised a barbecue for some of the drivers and teams, and Crystal couldn't help but feel excited at the prospect of hanging out with the teams.

Walking past the garage area and the line of haulers, Crystal spotted a tall, brown-haired man in a Maximus Motorsports uniform, walking next to Kent. She was positive it was Steve Grosso. She gave herself a mental pep talk, prepared to make a good impression. Once Steve met her—once she wasn't just a generic "younger woman" dating his dad—she was sure everything would be all right.

She glanced up at Larry. He squared his shoulders and increased his pace, walking straight toward the pair.

Steve spotted them, and annoyance flexed over his face.

Kent, on the other hand, smiled a greeting. But then

he glanced at their joined hands, and his eyes narrowed in puzzlement.

"Steve," Larry greeted, in a deep voice.

"Dad," came the tense-shouldered response.

Crystal put on her most friendly smile, while Larry turned his attention to Kent.

"Kent, I don't know if you remember Crystal Hayes?"

Kent gave her a nod of greeting. "Sure." His glance went to their joined hands again, clearly working through the possible scenarios.

"Crystal and I are dating," said Larry.

Steve's lips compressed, and his eyes narrowed at his father.

"Nice to see you again, Crystal," Kent put in conversationally.

"Good luck tomorrow," she offered, trying hard to ignore Steve's censure. This wasn't going nearly as well as she'd hoped.

"We're running late," said Steve in a clipped tone.

"You're not going to say hello to Crystal?" Larry asked his son.

The tone was as terse as his expression. "Hello, Crystal."

She forced herself to ignore the undercurrents. She wouldn't win him over by getting angry. "Hello, Steve."

Larry, however, didn't seem to be in the mood to let the slight pass. He took a step toward Steve, dropping his voice. "Don't be an ass."

"We're running late," Steve repeated.

"A radio call-in show," Kent added jovially, in an obvious attempt to defuse the tension.

"I hope it's fun," said Crystal, while father and son stared each other down.

"CJRM," said Kent, glancing at Steve.

"I know they have an affiliate in Charlotte," she tried.

But Kent had given up. He gaped openly at the other two men.

Crystal wrapped her hand around Larry's arm. "Larry, we should probably let them—"

"This isn't the way I raised you," Larry said to Steve.

"*Larry,*" Crystal tried again, tugging his arm. She hadn't expected things to go off the rails this quickly nor this completely.

Steve slid her a look of contempt.

"What?" she found herself asking.

"He thinks you're after my money," said Larry.

Steve's jaw dropped a quarter inch, and Kent took a step back.

"You *what?*" asked Crystal, too astonished to maintain her facade.

"Dad," Steve protested.

"We might as well put our cards on the table." Larry looked to Crystal. "Are you after my money?"

"Absolutely not." She crossed her arms over her chest and confronted Steve. "I'm after his body."

"This isn't a joke," he growled.

Kent grabbed Steve's arm and bodily moved him to one side. "We're late," he said with finality. "The rest of this is going to have to wait." Then he steered Steve around Larry and Crystal.

"See what I mean?" Larry said to Crystal as the two men disappeared. "People are going to assume the worst."

Steve hadn't even given Crystal a chance.

Larry took her hand again. "Steve and your mother," he sighed. "I'm waiting for Milo's reaction, as well as the rest of the family. Imagine what perfect strangers are going to say."

"I don't care," Crystal asserted. She truly didn't. She was willing to put up a fight for Larry. She had to believe that Steve would eventually calm down. Over time, he'd be forced to believe she wasn't after Larry's money.

As for the strangers? They were strangers. Who cared what they thought or said? But family…they could make it difficult.

Just then, three men dressed in orange and brown Fulcrum Racing uniforms walked by. They gazed at Larry, then their attention shifted to Crystal, then one nudged the other and made a sly-smiled comment.

Larry made a sound of frustration deep in his throat.

"I didn't even see that," said Crystal, pointedly looking straight ahead.

But it was frustrating to have her looks prejudice people's reactions all over again. With Simon, men had always given him automatic respect and a *lucky dog* smirk while she was on his arm. And he'd preened under the attention. With Larry, it was the opposite. It was clear people thought he'd somehow bought and paid for her.

"IT'S THE PRICE YOU PAY FOR a fifty-two second lap," said Dean, protecting his rib cage as he eased his body into a lawn chair on the rough grass outside his motor home. The awning provided shade from the waning sun, while a light breeze rustled the red-checked table cloth next to the stainless-steel propane barbecue.

"Will it bother you tomorrow?" asked crew chief, Perry Noble, helping himself to a soda from the cooler.

"Just a bruise," said Dean, his gaze resting on Larry and Crystal.

Crystal caught Patsy's profile as she set out chips and

salsa next to a fruit platter and smoothed the table cloth. Her movements were clipped and precise.

"Larry," Dean greeted. "Crystal."

Crystal glanced at Dean, expecting disapproval, so she wasn't surprised when it was there in his expression. But she was more worried about Patsy.

"I'm sorry you were hurt," she said to Dean.

"That's racing. Besides, it's nothing," said Dean, while Patsy marched back into the motor home.

Crystal took a chance and followed her. She rapped lightly on the metal door before gingerly pushing it open. "Patsy?"

Patsy turned from the sink that was halfway down the massive motor home. "Come in, Crystal."

"Everything okay?"

"Of course," she continued washing tomatoes, placing them on a tea towel beside the sink. "Dean got the pole."

"Fantastic."

"Yeah."

Crystal came inside, latching the door behind her. "Thanks for inviting us."

"Thanks for coming." Patsy swiped at her cheek with the back of her hand.

Crystal moved closer still. "You sure everything's okay?"

"Dean bruised his ribs."

"I saw that."

"No spinout, no crash, no nothing. Just a mishap with the harness, and he's got a bruised rib."

"Will he be able to drive tomorrow?"

Patsy gave a hollow laugh, yanking the plug from the sink and drying her hands on a corner of the towel. Her hands trembled ever so slightly. "The man could be in traction, and he'd be begging them to winch him into the driver's seat." She pulled open a drawer and retrieved a long, sharp knife.

Crystal moved in. "Why don't you let me do that?" She gently removed the knife from Patsy's hand.

"Am I that bad?" Patsy stared down at her trembling hands. "Damn." She pressed them against her beige shorts.

"Do you need a drink?" asked Crystal, washing her hands. "Maybe you should sit down."

"I would, if I thought it would help." Patsy crossed to the big refrigerator and retrieved a head of lettuce. "I hope you like hamburgers."

"I love hamburgers," said Crystal, slicing through the juicy tomatoes.

"How's Larry?"

"He's good." Crystal glanced out the window to where Larry had pulled a chair up next to Dean. The two men were talking with Perry who stood facing them.

"Any developments?"

Patsy looked like a nervous wreck, but Crystal was willing to go along with small talk if that's what she wanted.

"He's agreed to tell the world we're dating."

"Good."

"Yeah. Patsy—"

"I mean, there's nothing to hide, right?" Patsy's laugh was a little shrill.

Crystal reached out to cover Patsy's hand. "Does Dean know you're this upset?"

Patsy gazed at her with deep, luminous, blue eyes and then laughed again. "He thinks I'm being unreasonable and should seek psychological help."

Crystal laughed, too."

Patsy sighed. "I can't leave. But I can't stay."

Everything froze inside Crystal. "It's that serious?"

Patsy concentrated on the lettuce, but she gave a shaky nod. "We're fighting all the time. It's no good for me, and I can't let him drive off in his race car upset. Can you imagine…"

Crystal wrapped an arm around Patsy's narrow shoulders. Her gaze went to the window once again, taking in the man whose stubbornness was making Patsy miserable.

Perry was gone, and she could tell from Larry's and Dean's arm gestures that they were arguing.

"What do you want to do?" Crystal whispered to Patsy.

"The impossible," said Patsy. "But what I'll do instead, is be a good NASCAR wife. I'll swallow my fear and support my husband. He's got an important race tomorrow, and he needs to focus. That's the best—" Her voice broke, but she quickly regrouped. "Thanks."

"For what?" asked Crystal. She hadn't done a single thing to help. She didn't even have any advice for Patsy.

"For listening," said Patsy. "It helps."

"I'm glad. But…" She looked pointedly out of the window at the two angry men. "It might have been better if Larry and I had stayed away."

Patsy followed the direction of her gaze. "He's definitely not thrilled with your relationship," she agreed.

"Has he said anything?" asked Crystal, girding herself.

"He's said a lot of things. Most of them you don't need to hear. I'm honestly not sure if he's that convinced Larry is making a fool of himself, or if Dean's grown so accustomed to seeing Larry alone, that he's worried about him. The Grossos are extremely close. They protect each other."

"Larry's not making a fool of himself," Crystal quickly defended. "And don't worry. I like him. A lot. And that's all there is to it."

Patsy nodded. "I believe you."

"I don't try to look like a trophy girlfriend."

Patsy pulled back and took in Crystal's plain white T-shirt, sensible shoes, her simple ponytail and minuscule makeup. "I know you don't."

"I wish I was forty, with wrinkles. Maybe a little gray hair."

Patsy laughed. "No, you don't."

"Okay, maybe that is a bit too radical. But it would sure make this situation a lot easier."

"Relationships are never easy," said Patsy.

Crystal sighed. Patsy was a wise woman. If she and Dean were still struggling, what chance did Crystal and Larry stand?

CHAPTER THIRTEEN

WHEN HE SAW CRYSTAL AND Patsy exiting the motor home, Larry turned up the volume on the radio. Kent was doing a good job with the call-in show, and Larry hoped it would distract his brother from their argument. He'd wanted Crystal to be confronted with the reality of his family's reaction to their relationship, but enough was enough.

"You can delude yourself all you want," said Dean, cranking the radio back down and keeping his voice to a low growl. "But if you care about her, and if you're half a man, you'll walk away."

Out of earshot, Crystal smiled at Larry as she walked down the short steps, arms laden with food for the barbecue. He returned the smile, but he didn't like what Dean was saying. And he sure didn't like the sense it was making inside his brain.

"You're not what she needs," Dean continued. "And you know it. Otherwise, we wouldn't be having this conversation. You'd have punched my lights out ten minutes ago."

Larry didn't answer his brother. Instead he stared straight ahead and tried to pretend that Dean wasn't right, that Dean wasn't echoing the doubts that had been inside Larry's head for the past two weeks.

After a long minute's silence, Dean cranked the radio back up, and Kent's voice filled the air.

"The folks at Maximus Motorsports and Vittle Farms have done an outstanding job of supporting the team this year. And the No. 427 team just keeps getting better and better. I don't know if you saw my pit stops in Dover, Tammy, but we didn't lose a second in the pits."

"Well, I saw those Dover pits stops," came the host's voice. "And your crew was on fire. Our next caller is from Boise, Idaho. Go ahead, Jack."

"Great to talk to you, Kent," said the caller.

"Hello there, Jack," came Kent's jovial reply.

"Can you talk a bit about family rivalry? I see your Dad's got the pole position for tomorrow's race. How does that play into your strategy?"

"We'll be chasing Dad and the No. 414 car along with everybody else. He may be wily, but I'm eager, and I don't plan to be in his rearview mirror for long." Then Kent's voice got more serious. "The Cargill Motorsports team is having a phenomenal year, and I've no doubt it's going to be a great race."

"What about rumors of his retirement?" asked the host.

"You'll have to talk to Dad on that one," said Kent.

The host left a split second of dead air, then obviously accepted that Kent wouldn't say anything further.

"He's doing a good job," Larry said to Dean.

Dean nodded. He was a veteran of many interviews, and he obviously knew they could get tricky, particularly when they were live.

"Next caller. We have Patrick from Charlotte. A hometown fan."

"Hello, Kent?" came the caller.

"Hi there," said Kent.

"I know there's a lot of money involved in NASCAR. I wonder if you worry about scam artists." The caller paused.

"I don't follow you," said Kent.

"Gold diggers," explained the caller, his voice going hard. "Who take up, for example, with your uncle, who should know better than to be conned by a young, pretty face."

There was a moment of stunned silence, both on the air and at the barbecue. Larry met Crystal's gaze and saw the hurt in her green eyes.

He swore under his breath, rising from his chair to go to her.

"If you're suggesting some of the team's wives and girlfriends are beautiful," Kent's voice followed him, "I'd have to agree with you. My fiancée, Tanya, for example is a knockout. Love you, honey. And my spotter's new fiancée could stop traffic—even at 180 miles an hour. As for the money in NASCAR, I think it's a well-documented fact that racing is expensive. That's why we appreciate the support of sponsors like Vittle Farms and, of course, Dawson Ritter and Maximus Motorsports. We couldn't race without them."

"We have to take a short break," the announcer put in. "For some words from one of *our* favorite sponsors."

"That was outrageous," Patsy hissed.

Crystal's lower lip trembled, but she put on a smile. "Kent did a great job deflecting. We'll have to thank him for that. You have a very intelligent son."

Larry drew Crystal into his arms. "I'm so sorry."

"No worries," she said, pulling back, and turning her attention to the table, brushing off some imaginary dust and straightening a fold that didn't need straightening.

"Why do people have to fixate on age?" said Patsy vehemently.

"You're joking," came Dean's dry voice as he joined them, opening the barbecue and picking up a pack of matches.

Patsy glared a warning at her husband.

He glared right back. "You've done *nothing* but fixate on my age for months."

Larry was too stunned to immediately react. His brother and sister-in-law looked genuinely furious.

"Not now," Patsy said, and Larry snagged Crystal's elbow, easing her away from the married couple.

Dean slammed down the barbecue lid.

Patsy glanced around at the group of people studiously concentrating on other things. Obviously mortified, she fled into the motor home.

"Should I go after her?" Crystal asked Larry in a worried voice.

"Probably give her a minute." He tilted his head to look at Crystal. "You okay?"

"Fine."

"We should talk about this."

"About what?"

He drew a sigh. "Don't play dumb with me. I know your IQ, remember?"

"It's one wing nut's opinion. Patsy's the one with the real problem."

Larry sat down on a lawn chair, drawing Crystal sideways between his knees. "We can talk about it later."

She crouched down to perch on his thigh, sending him a smoldering gaze. "Talking's not what I'd planned to do later."

IT WAS AN EMOTIONAL WEEKEND for Crystal and everybody else. Kent took third in the Pocono race, while Dean settled for fourth. Dean barely missed being caught up in a Bart Branch instigated pileup, which probably upset Patsy. She left the track before the end of the race.

By the time Crystal realized she was gone, it was too late to go after her, and nobody heard from her before Crystal and Larry packed up for home.

Saturday night had been glorious in Larry's arms, but he'd been strangely quiet all day Sunday. And now, pulling up to Crystal's staircase, he shut off the engine and angled his body to face her in the car.

"I promised myself I'd do this before I dropped you off," he said.

She swiveled to face him, bracing her back against the car door, making out his face in the stark white of the parking lot lights. "Do what?"

"I think…" He paused and pulled his hand over his chin. "I think we need to stop seeing each other."

Crystal's stomach plummeted, and her entire world shifted beneath her. "What?" she barely rasped, desperately hoping she'd misunderstood.

But he nodded his head. "I've been giving this a lot of thought." He choked out a self-deprecating laugh. "A hell of a lot of thought."

Crystal struggled to understand his bombshell. "Is this because of the call-in show?"

"It's because of a lot of things."

"The guy was a judgmental jerk."

"But he hurt you."

"He didn't hurt me," she protested. "He's a total stranger."

"I saw it in your eyes," said Larry.

"You were thirty feet away."

He gripped the steering wheel, focusing out the windshield. "I'm not the right guy for you."

Real fear gripped Crystal. "Yes," she insisted. "You are."

He shook his head. "You want children."

"Not that badly."

He looked at her again. "You *deserve* children. I've seen you with Jennifer and David, and you'll make a great mother."

"And you make a great father. That doesn't mean—"

"I am a father. That's the difference."

Crystal stared in silence at his implacable face. This couldn't be happening. He couldn't do this to her. She loved him. She was completely and desperately in love with him, and she couldn't imagine her life going forward any other way.

"I don't understand," she tried.

"I love you," he said.

She shook her head in denial. "If you loved me—"

"*Because* I love you, I'm walking away. I'm not what you need."

"You're exactly what I need."

He reached for her hand across the dim front seat. "You need someone younger. Someone in the same space of life as you."

She gave a cold laugh, yanking her hand away from his. If she was forced to endure his gentle touch, she'd burst into tears. She had to stay strong here. She had to somehow convince him he was wrong.

"And what space of life is that?" she asked.

"Starting a family, not finishing one off."

She felt a spurt of anger. "Is that how you see yourself? Finishing off."

"I'm fifty years old."

"Yeah, you're fifty, not eighty-five."

"Crystal."

"Don't Crystal me. There are two of us in this relationship. It's not all up to you."

"It's for your own good."

"If you loved me, you would fight *for* me."

"I *am* fighting for you. And the person I'm fighting is *me.* I'm walking away so that you can have the life you deserve. If you think this is easy for me—"

Panic clawed at her chest. "Then don't do it."

"I have to do it."

"No." She shook her head frantically. "You don't."

Larry took a deep breath. "You'll thank me—"

Anger overcame everything else. "I will *never* thank you. Leave me if you have to, but don't pretend it's for me. There's no younger version of you waiting on the next street corner. There's you and there's me, or there's nothing at all."

He reached for her again, but she shrank back.

"That's simply not true," he told her. "There'll be other men."

"Other men? You can actually visualize me with *other men?*"

Something flashed in his eyes. Sorrow, hurt, rage? She couldn't tell. But it changed instantly to determination. "If I stay, then I'm a selfish son of a bitch."

The fight went out of her, and tears threatened. "You truly believe that?"

His hands twisted convulsively on the steering wheel. "I know that."

"You're wrong." Her voice nearly broke.

He shook his head. "You'll thank me, Crystal. I know you will."

Her eyes burned, and she was forced to blink rapidly. He thought he was saving her, and there was no way to talk him out of it. She stared into his eyes, remembering last night, remembering every single, joyous moment they'd had together.

"Don't do this," she pleaded.

He gazed lovingly into her eyes, and she thought she had him. He remembered. He got it. He knew they were meant for each other.

But his voice broke, and he answered her. "I have to."

She closed her eyes, while the world spun. Groping blindly, she clutched at the door handle. Her overnight bag was in the back, but she didn't care. She had to get out of the car, and she had to do it now.

She wrenched open the door and fled up the stairs.

Tears streaming down her cheeks, Crystal didn't look back. Her hand shook as she inserted the key into the lock.

Her phone was ringing in the kitchen, and for one wild, optimistic moment, she thought it might be Larry's cell, that he'd changed his mind, that he was calling her back.

But Amber's number flashed on the screen.

"No," she wailed. *Not now. Please, not now.*

But she picked up the call. It could be Jennifer. Or something might be wrong.

She took a breath. "Hello?"

"Crystal? Oh, Crystal. Where have you been?"

"What's wrong?"

"I called and called," said Amber, a slur apparent in her voice. "I needed to talk to you," she hiccupped.

"Where are you?" asked Crystal. "Where are the kids?"

"I'm home," Amber sang. "They're sleeping."

"Are you sure? Are they all right?"

"I'm sure." Amber gave a big sigh. "I had a fight with Zane. He left."

Crystal couldn't help the surge of relief. "Did he leave town?"

"I think so." The tears came back into Amber's voice. "Oh, Crystal. I'm so messed up."

Crystal swiped at her own tears with the back of her hand, ripping a tissue from the box and crossing to her couch. "Are you hurt?"

"I'm sorry."

"Did he hit you?"

"Who?"

"Zane."

"Uh, no. I don't think so." Something rustled in the background. "I don't see anything."

"You *can't remember?*" Crystal cringed. This was worse than she thought. "Are you sure the kids are okay?"

The couch springs squeaked. "I'm walking—oops." Amber giggled. "I'm walking to the bedroom."

"Don't wake them up," Crystal warned.

"Shh," Amber slurred into the phone.

"Sound asleep," she announced.

"Both of them?"

"Uh-huh. They're so beautiful. My babies."

"Yes, they are," Crystal agreed. "And they need you."

"They need me." A sob escaped from Amber's throat. "I'm not a good mommy."

"You're a fine mommy." Sometimes. Most of the time. At least when Zane wasn't in town.

"I'm not," Amber disagreed. "But you're great. You're the best auntie in the world."

Her words were close enough to Larry's that Crystal's chest started to burn. Larry was gone. He was out of her life, and she had to find a way to carry on.

"You should sleep," she managed to say around the lump in her throat.

"I can't sleep. I'm so messed up, Crystal."

It was the second time Amber had used that phrase, and a horrible thought crept into Crystal's mind.

"You didn't do anything… Uh, something other than alcohol, did you?"

"A little weed."

"Amber!"

"Just a little. I was sooo…" She drew out the word. "Zane wanted to, and he was mad. Oh, Crystal. He's mad. He left. He said…"

Crystal battled the urge to rush over to her sister's house. But the kids were asleep, and Zane was gone. And if her state was anything to go by, Amber would soon fall asleep as well. Jennifer had her own cell phone. She'd call if she needed help.

"Amber?"

"Do you think I'm stupid?"

"No, honey. You're not stupid. You need to get some sleep. We can talk in the morning."

"Zane says I am."

"Zane is stupid. And he's gone. Did you lock your door?"

"Isss locked."

"You're sure?"

"Yep."

"Check for me, okay?"

"I'm standing up—whoops—again."

The sound of fumbling and tapping came through the phone.

"All locked up," said Amber.

"The deadbolt and chain?"

"Yep."

"Good."

More rustling. "I love you, Crystal."

"I love you, too. I'll call you in the morning."

"He's gone," Amber sighed.

"That's a good thing," said Crystal. "You don't need him. I want you to lie down."

"Lying down. He's gone." And her voice faded away.

"He's gone," Crystal repeated, thinking of Larry, hitting the off button on the phone. Her eyes instantly welled up with fresh tears.

AT FOUR IN THE MORNING, Larry was a raw mass of pain. He knew he'd done the right thing, but he also knew that if he stuck around Charlotte, he'd be rushing back to Crystal, begging for her forgiveness before the day was out.

He threw some clothes into his suitcase, sent an e-mail to his assistant, asking him to stop by and water the plants, then he checked the weather report to make sure he could land at Myrtle Pond.

His cell phone rang and, for a frightening moment, he thought it was Crystal. He hated the way his heart lifted, and he knew he wouldn't have the strength to tell her goodbye a second time. But it was his brother's number on the display. Dean, who knew full well Larry was always up by four.

He pressed the talk button. "What's up?"

Dean's voice was hoarse. "You haven't, by any chance, heard from Patsy?"

"What?"

"She never came back to the track. And she didn't come home last night."

Patsy would normally take the team plane back to Charlotte. But if she was avoiding Dean, she might have found another way home.

"Maybe she's on her way," said Larry. "Maybe she booked a commercial flight."

"Yeah," said Dean. "That's probably it."

"Did you try her cell?"

"I left a few messages."

"Dean," Larry paused. "How bad is this?"

His brother was silent for a few beats. "I think she might have left me."

"For refusing to retire?" That didn't sound like Patsy.

"I said some things to her Saturday night." Another pause. "It was our biggest fight. Ever. We both lost our tempers…"

Larry stepped back in. "Maybe she just needs a day or so. She loves you."

"Maybe," said Dean, but he didn't sound convinced. "Will you call me? If you hear from her?"

"Of course," said Larry. "Have you talked to Kent?"

"Yeah. We're trying to keep this quiet. We don't want the tabloids getting wind of it. Do you mind checking with Crystal? She and Patsy seemed close on the weekend."

Larry hesitated. "That's not a real good idea."

"Why? Is she there? If she's there—"

"I can't call Crystal."

"Why not?"

"Because we broke up last night."

There was silence on the other end. "You—"

"Don't say a thing," Larry warned. "Not a thing. I'm going to Myrtle Pond for a few days. I'll call you if I hear from Patsy."

"Thanks. Larry?"

"Yeah?"

"Hang in there."

Larry shut off the phone.

He pictured Crystal's laughing face.

He could get in his car. Drive to her house. Get down

on his knees and beg her forgiveness. Tell her he'd stay with her every day, hour and minute if she'd let him.

Or he could fly to Myrtle Pond and let her find another man and get on with her life.

His hands curled into fists. He clenched his jaw. Then he cursed a blue streak while slamming the lid down on his suitcase.

CRYSTAL SLEPT FITFULLY FROM five until eight. Rufus, drawn by her sobs, had parked himself on the foot of her bed. She woke up with red, puffy eyes and a throbbing headache, having spent most of the night alternating between missing Larry and examining the sorry state of her life.

In the wee hours, she'd come to the conclusion she was as bad as Amber, pinning her aspirations and self-worth on a man. She suddenly realized she'd been living in limbo for years, ever since Simon died. Not that her future had stretched out rosy with Simon; she truly would have divorced him. But afterward, she might also have pulled herself up by her bootstraps.

What did she think she was doing? Living above her parents' business, flitting from writing to parts driving and back again? There was a very real possibility Jennifer and David were going to need her again soon. That meant she had to be in a position to take care of them. And it could be for weeks or months this time.

She could no longer afford to drift through life.

She'd cataloged her weaknesses, which were many. And Larry was going to be a hollow ache in her body for a long time to come.

But then she'd catalogued her strengths. She was smart—her IQ told her that. She was fairly well organized. She could write. She could drive. And she was a darn decent pet owner.

In fact, Rufus had taught her just how much she loved animals. She was kind and compassionate. And she did have five million dollars to play with. Plus, she had Simon's pension and life insurance. It had mounted up to nearly one hundred thousand dollars. If the kids needed Simon's money, she'd use it.

But, more than just money, she needed to get some focus in her life. Her writing had slipped of late. Maybe she brought that back as a focus, or maybe if she had a proper career, maybe then losing Larry wouldn't hurt so badly.

The only thing she knew for sure was that she had to try something. Sitting around feeling sorry for herself wasn't going to cut it.

She rolled herself out of bed, heading for the shower, trying to rinse away the gritty sting from her eyes. Then she made herself a proper breakfast—bacon, eggs and homemade pancakes.

She'd call Fred Smythe this morning, get things rolling on the charitable trust.

And then it hit her.

She dropped her fork and stared at Rufus.

The trust. It would take planning and organization. Somebody would have to run the foundation, decide where to put the money, pick priorities, decide who to hire. There was no reason in the world it couldn't be her.

And that meant she could collect a salary, get a bigger apartment, maybe one close to Jennifer and David's school. That way, if they needed her, now or anytime, she'd be there.

Against all odds, she felt a smile form on her lips. She could find ways to help more dogs like Rufus and cats and birds. And she could work from home—write when she had time, sleep in, work evenings, whatever she wanted to do.

Crystal stood up from her chair. She had a proper job. She could get her own apartment and stand on her own two feet.

It was about bloody time.

CHAPTER FOURTEEN

FRED SMYTHE HAD enthusiastically engaged in the animal foundation project. Crystal spent the next few days mired in the incredible details of setting up the trust, and the next few nights painfully missing Larry. He was wrong to leave her. She wasn't going to find another man. In twenty-eight years, even with Simon, she hadn't truly fallen in love. And now that she knew what it felt like, she wouldn't settle for anything less.

It was late now, after eleven. She squinted at the Humane Society bylaws in front of her. She didn't want to duplicate their services, but she did want to learn from their experiences.

Her cell phone rang.

As always, her heart leapt at the thought of Larry changing his mind. But after three days, and three very long nights, she knew that wasn't going to happen. In fact, she'd known that wasn't going to happen the second she'd looked into his eyes and he'd told her he was doing it for her.

Ironic, really, the thing that made her love him the most—his integrity—was also the thing that meant they'd never be together.

Her phone chimed again, and she glanced at the readout. Her heart clunked in her chest.

Jennifer.

She scrambled to answer it.

"Sweetheart? Are you all right?"

"Auntie Crystal?" came a shaking voice. Crystal could hear David crying in the background, and something was roaring above Jennifer's voice.

"What is it? Are you all right? Where are you?" Crystal forced herself to take a breath.

"We crashed," Jennifer whimpered.

"Crashed what? The car?" Panic clawed its way into Crystal's throat, and she rose to her feet, marching compulsively toward the door. Rufus immediately followed.

"Yes," said Jennifer, tears in her voice.

"Is that David? Is he okay? Who's with you?"

"David's crying!"

"Is he hurt?"

"I don't know…. It's dark."

"Where's Mommy?"

Jennifer was silent as the engine roar and a country station rose around her.

"Mommy's not moving."

Crystal's entire body went cold. "Was she driving?"

"My dad was driving."

Zane.

"Where is he now?" asked Crystal, anger moving in on her rising terror.

Jennifer's voice was hoarse. "He left us. He got out of the car and ran away!"

"Do you know where you are, honey? Can you see any lights or street signs?"

"We fell down a hill."

Oh, God. Crystal's throat closed over. "Tell me what you see?"

"We're upside down!"

Crystal bit down on her index finger to keep from whimpering. Rufus snaked around her legs, pressing against her.

"I see the dashboard. It's raining."

Crystal glanced out her window. Raining here. Probably raining all over Charlotte.

"There's a flashing light!"

"On the dashboard?"

"Outside…. Up by the road."

"The police?" Crystal's heart gave a leap.

"I think so."

"Can you see any people? Are they coming down the hill? Is David still crying?" Crystal clenched her jaw, forcing herself to quit peppering Jennifer with questions.

"They have flashlights," said Jennifer, sounding calmer.

"And David?"

"He's crying quieter. It's okay, David. I see the policeman. He's coming to help us."

Tears flowed freely down Crystal's cheeks. "Has Mommy moved?" she asked.

"No," Jennifer whispered.

"Honey, can you do something for me?"

"Yes," the girl's voice wobbled.

"When a grown-up gets there. A policeman or a fireman. Can you give him the phone? Make sure you tell him I'm your auntie?"

"Here he comes," said Jennifer. "I think it's a policeman." Her voice went quieter. "Can you talk to my Auntie Crystal?"

A man's voice came on the phone. "This is Officer Davis."

"My name is Crystal Hayes. Jennifer and David are my

niece and nephew. My sister is in the car, and her name is Amber. Can you tell me how she's doing? Are the kids okay?" Crystal prayed hard that Amber was still alive.

"I'd recommend you meet us at Memorial Hospital," said Officer Davis.

"Can you—"

"I'm sorry, ma'am. I have to attend to the accident."

"Is she alive?" Crystal wailed.

"She's unconscious," the man told her.

Somebody shouted for a backboard, and David started crying again.

"Memorial Hospital," said the officer, and the phone went dead.

Crystal scrambled for her shoes. Rufus stuck to her like glue, so she loaded him in the passenger seat of the car. She drove as fast as she dared through the pouring rain, tensing up at red lights, then cursing the crowded parking lot at the hospital.

She left Rufus in the car and flew across the parking lot to the emergency entrance. There was an ambulance outside, and she slowed her steps in horror as they unloaded her sister. Amber's hair was matted, her face was streaked with blood, and three different IVs swung from poles on the stretcher.

Crystal rushed forward, taking her sister's cold, damp hand. "Amber?"

Amber blinked her glazed eyes.

"I'm here, honey."

"Crystal," she breathed. "The kids?"

Crystal had no idea how the kids were doing. She glanced around, but couldn't see them anywhere. "I talked to Jennifer. They seem okay."

Amber cracked a very weak smile.

The doors whooshed open, and Crystal paced along inside, unsure how long they'd let her keep talking. Already a nurse was checking the IV, and people were shouting instructions.

"Take care…" Amber whispered. "The kids… Please."

Crystal's eyes welled up with fresh tears. "Of course I'll take care of the kids."

"Ma'am," said the nurse, touching Crystal's arm.

"They can stay with me as long as they need."

"I love them," Amber whispered, tears appearing in her green eyes.

"Ma'am," the nurse said more firmly. She pointed to a set of double doors coming up in the pathway. "You can't go through there."

Crystal stopped, taking one last look at her sister as she disappeared in a flurry of white coats and rushing feet.

"Crystal Hayes?" came a deep voice from behind her.

Wiping her eyes with a rain-wet hand, she turned to face a police officer.

"Are you Crystal Hayes?" he repeated.

She nodded, and he motioned to a small alcove in the hallway.

"I'm Officer Davis. Can we talk over here?"

"Is she…" Crystal began, then swallowed. "Do you…" But she couldn't bring herself to voice the question. "Are the kids okay?"

The policeman nodded and adjusted his cap where it was tucked under his arm. "The children are with a doctor. So far, it looks like bruises only."

Crystal staggered back with a wave of relief.

Officer Davis quickly grabbed her arm. "Are you okay, ma'am?"

Crystal nodded.

He opened a little notebook. "What can you tell me about a Zane Crandell?"

Other than the fact that he's about to die by my hand? "He's my sister's ex-husband. Jennifer, my niece, said he was driving."

"When you talked to her on the phone?"

"Yes."

"Do you know where he lives? The places he hangs out?"

"I think he still lives in Atlanta. I don't know where he was staying in Charlotte."

"We're concerned about some of the things the children told us."

Crystal raised her eyebrows.

"It sounds like Zane made some threats against both their mother and them."

Crystal felt her blood pressure rise. "What kind of threats?"

"Does Zane drink?" asked the officer.

"All the time. What were the threats?"

"Regarding their physical safety. Until he's caught, we think it would be best—"

"Crystal?" came her mother's voice as her parents appeared in the hallway.

"I saw her for a minute," said Crystal as they drew close. "I haven't talked to the doctor yet. She's hurt." Her voice broke. "Pretty bad."

Her mother glanced around, motioning for her father to follow her to the nurses' station.

Crystal watched them for a moment, then turned back to the officer, gathering her strength from deep inside her. "What do you need?"

"Understand this is an abundance of caution. But do

you have somewhere to take the children? Not to your house. Preferably somewhere unknown to Zane Crandell."

Crystal immediately thought of Larry. "Yes."

"We're fairly certain he has bigger things to worry about at the moment, but…"

"I understand. Thank you, Officer."

The man nodded and flipped his little book closed.

Crystal headed for her parents at the nurses' station.

Her father looked pale in creased shorts and a rumpled T-shirt, but her mother was her usual, controlled, no-nonsense self. "They're taking her into surgery," she told Crystal. "The children are fine, and we should know something more in a few hours."

She marched to a set of plastic chairs lined up along the wall.

Crystal took a seat beside her mother. "They've asked me to take the children."

Her mother patted her knee. "That's a good idea. We'll stay here with Amber. There'll be paperwork and things to fill out. We can get it done before she wakes up."

"Mom?" Crystal couldn't figure out if her mother was the Rock of Gibraltar, or simply in denial.

Her mother looked at her, face composed, no hint of emotion. The same way she'd looked through every crisis Crystal could remember. Maybe it was for the best. Maybe worrying wouldn't help any.

"I think I'll take the kids to Larry's." Crystal was certain Larry would say yes. "It sounds like Zane's out of control."

There was a flicker of something deep in her mother's eyes. But she didn't say anything, simply gave a sharp nod of acquiescence.

Crystal stood up and pulled out her phone.

She dialed Larry's home number. But when there was no answer there, she dialed his cell.

"Larry Grosso," was his quick response.

"Larry, it's Crystal."

The announcement was met with silence.

She heard music in the background.

"I'm sorry to bother you," she began, hoping he wasn't on a date or something equally embarrassing.

"No problem," he said. "Nash and I are having a beer."

He was at Myrtle Pond. Her heart sank.

"Crystal?"

"There's…uh…"

A page came over the speaker, and she walked a little ways down the hall, hoping for more quiet.

"Where are you?" Larry asked.

"At the hospital."

"What—"

"It's Amber. There was a car accident. Zane."

Larry swore. Then he mumbled something.

"What did you say?"

"I just told Nash."

Crystal took a deep breath. "Listen. I thought you'd be in town. Amber's going into surgery, and the police want me to take the kids someplace Zane doesn't know."

Larry's tone went dark. "Why?"

"He ran from the accident, and he's made some threats."

More mumbling, then his tone went crisp. "Are the kids with you?"

"They're here. They're scared and bruised, but the policeman thinks they're okay. They're being looked at right now by doctors."

"Hang on a second. Nash wants to talk to you."

Confused, Crystal waited.

"Crystal?"

"Nash?"

"Here's what we're going to do."

We?

"Take the kids, and drive straight to the airport," said Nash. "Don't go anywhere but the passenger drop-off zone. There'll be a security guard waiting there to meet you."

"A what?"

"A security guard."

"But—"

"Go with him. He'll take you to meet Larry." There was a clattering sound.

"The police don't think there's any real danger."

"And I'm sure they're right. Larry and I are on our way to the airstrip right now to get the Cessna."

"Crystal?" It was Larry's voice again.

"I don't understand." They weren't running for their lives, simply taking an extra precaution.

"Do what Nash told you," Larry said. "I'll be on the ground in Charlotte in half an hour."

Jennifer and David appeared at the far end of the hall. A nurse was between them, holding their hands. They looked tiny, pale and vulnerable. And she suddenly wanted to get them as far away from their bastard father as humanly possible.

"I've got the kids," she said into the phone.

"Good. Straight to the car. Straight to the airport, and go with the security guy."

"Right."

"See you soon."

Crystal dropped to one knee and opened her arms.

Jennifer and David rushed in, and she held them tight.

"You were so brave," she told Jennifer. "You did everything exactly right."

"They chopped my shirt off with scissors," said David, holding his arm to show off a hospital smock.

"They wanted to make sure you weren't hurt," said Crystal, struggling to keep the emotion out of her voice. She didn't want to scare them any more than they already were.

"Mommy?" asked Jennifer in a quiet voice, slipping an arm around her brother's shoulders.

Crystal drew back to look them both in the eyes. "Mommy needs to have an operation."

They nodded gravely, then they glanced up to see their grandparents.

Crystal's father engulfed each of the kids in a warm hug, while her mother efficiently checked them over for anything the medical staff might have missed.

"How would you guys like to go see Uncle Larry at Myrtle Pond?" Crystal asked.

David's face lit up. "In the airplane?"

Crystal nodded.

"Yeah," said David.

"Are we sleeping over?" asked Jennifer.

Crystal nodded. "Grandma and Grandpa are going to stay here with Mommy, and I'm going to take care of you two for a few days. That okay?"

"Did Mommy wake up?" asked Jennifer.

"I talked to her for a couple of minutes before she went in to see the doctor. She said to tell you she loves you." Crystal was forced to turn away before Jennifer could see her tears.

Her father was quick to distract the children, gathering them against his broad chest. "Give me a hug goodbye."

Then he met her gaze above the kids' heads. He was worried. She was worried, too. She tried to be like her mother, but a sick feeling of dread wormed its way through her system. She indulged herself in ten seconds of complete despair, then she forced herself to rally.

"Rufus is waiting in the car," she told the kids, taking their hands. "We might have to run through the rain."

As they headed down the hall, she turned back to mouth the words "call me" to her parents. She didn't doubt they would. But it made her feel better to clarify the request.

When they got to the main doors of the emergency department, a young police officer fell into step with them.

"Are you heading for the parking lot, ma'am?"

Crystal nodded.

"I'll walk along with you."

Maybe it was the officer's presence, but an eerie feeling crept along Crystal's spine as she hustled the kids through the dark rain. She was glad when they were in the car—doors locked, engine running and Rufus taking a post next to David.

When she drove up to the drop-off zone at the airport, three men in black vests, with SECURITY emblazoned in yellow across their backs, all but swarmed her vehicle. One took the keys and whisked the car away. The other two guided them, Rufus and all, to a private lounge. There, one of the men stayed outside the door while the other introduced himself to the kids, chatting cheerfully while he showed them a small side counter with muffins, fruit and soft drinks.

A few minutes later, the security guard who'd taken the car showed up. He gave Crystal the keys and produced a new T-shirt for David. It was a bright blue tourist special, with North Carolina embroidered across the chest. But David was thrilled.

When Larry walked through the door, Crystal felt a rush of relief. He hugged both the kids.

"You guys okay?" he asked them.

"We wore our seat belts," said David. "Just like jet fighter pilots."

She met Larry's gaze, and her gratitude nearly staggered her. Amber hadn't been wearing her seat belt. Who knew if she would have insisted the kids wear theirs?

A split second later, Crystal was wrapped in Larry's arms. She all but melted against his strength, feeling like she could finally share the load of emotion.

Too soon, he was easing back from her. "Anybody been in an airplane at night?" he asked the kids.

"Not me," said David.

Jennifer shook her head.

"Then you're in for a treat." He ushered them toward the door.

LARRY'S ADRENALINE WAS STILL at a steady hum when they got the kids to sleep around two o'clock. Closing the door of Nash's upstairs bedroom, he had to stop himself from taking Crystal in his arms. It was bad enough when she wasn't around, but with her here—and beautiful, and vulnerable and hurt—it was almost more than he could do to keep his emotions in check.

"Your bedroom's next door," he pointed to another doorway. "Bathroom's at the end."

"What about you?" she asked, those wide green eyes gazing at him in the soft light.

"I'll be downstairs."

Nash's bedroom was on the main floor, and Larry was going to take the pullout couch. He could have gone to his own house next door. The odds of Zane showing up in

Myrtle Pond were astronomically low, but Larry couldn't shake the instinct to put himself between Crystal and the kids, and any potential danger, no matter how remote.

"You want a drink or something?" he asked.

"I think I'll go straight to bed."

He nodded, but his mind was straying to thoughts of crawling into bed beside her and drawing her sweet body up against his own, wrapping her in his strength and working like hell to make her feel better, if only for a little while.

"Anything more from your parents?"

She shook her head. "They expected the surgery to take hours. She has some broken ribs, but they're most worried about…" She raised trembling fingers to her mouth. "Internal bleeding, and the head wound."

He took her hand, almost desperate to hold her, but terrified he wouldn't be able to let her go. "You call me if you hear?"

"I will."

"And let me know if you need anything. Anything at all."

The depths of her eyes told him what she needed, but it was the one thing he couldn't give her. Now wasn't the time to flaunt logic. Decisions made under emotional duress were inherently dangerous. A powerful hormonal cocktail was at work in his body, dilating his blood vessels, heightening everything he was thinking or feeling, making even insignificant issues seem of paramount importance.

If ever there was a time to let cooler heads prevail, this was it. And he'd had a cooler head on Sunday. He had to trust that he'd made a good decision then.

He let go of her hands. "I'll see you in the morning."

She nodded, and he turned to head down the stairs.

Nash was typing on his computer, a headset on one ear, his voice low into the microphone.

He spotted Larry, then turned to search the room, obviously checking for Crystal.

"Roger that," he said into the microphone. "Call me when you know."

Then he leaned back in his wheeled desk chair. "Got a few friends lending a hand with the police in Charlotte."

"I like your friends," said Larry, taking a seat nearby.

"They'd like you, too. They're following up on a couple of leads, checking out the local bars and hospitals. It looks like Zane left enough blood at the scene to test for blood alcohol. The jerk was plastered."

"Yet he tosses his own kids in the backseat for a joyride. The man ought to be shot."

"You serious?"

No, Larry wasn't serious. "We can hardly hunt him down and shoot him."

Nash slid his mouse pointer across the screen and clicked on an icon. "Apprehension mishaps happen all the time, my friend."

"I'd settle for a long stint in a detestable prison."

"Odds are with you, then."

LATE AFTERNOON, Crystal stood at the rail of Nash's deck watching Larry tow the kids on an inflatable raft behind Nash's speedboat. Amber had come through the surgery well, but she would be in intensive care for the foreseeable future. She'd also have months of therapy ahead of her for a shattered ankle and a broken pelvis.

She hadn't regained consciousness yet, which was probably a blessing. It was going to be a long, painful haul, and the best they could hope for was one day at a time.

They'd glossed over the details to the kids, and Larry had spent the past two days valiantly distracting them with games, water sports and renovation projects on the Victorian house. They'd even taken a shopping trip into Asheboro to pick up a few clothes.

Nash appeared next to her, handing her a glass of iced tea. She hadn't even heard him approach.

"Thanks," she told him, taking the cool, slippery glass.

He gave her a nod in response.

"And thanks for the security guards at the airport. I didn't realize how rattled I was that night."

"Not unusual," he said.

It wasn't the first time Nash had piqued her curiosity. "How would you know that?"

"You're human."

She supposed that was true enough.

"You did everything right," he assured her.

"Thanks."

The outboard motor whined as Larry made a turn, David squealed as he came flying off the inflatable raft, skimming the surface before bobbing under for a split second then being righted by his bright orange lifejacket.

He waved his arms, giving a thumbs-up.

Hanging on tightly to the inflatable herself, Jennifer shouted, "We're coming around for you!"

"He sure knows how to show them a good time," said Crystal, wishing for the thousandth time she was ten years older or Larry was ten years younger.

"You going to be okay?" asked Nash in a gruff voice.

She looked up at him for clarification.

"Spending time with him. Like this. While he stomps all over your heart?"

"He's not stomping—"

"Maybe not intentionally. But I see the way you look at him."

Crystal felt an embarrassed flush rise in her face. Pity from a man like Nash was really hard to take.

"It's the kids that count," she said.

"Agreed. But you have to live with the aftermath."

She swirled the iced tea and ice cubes. "I have a plan."

There was amusement in his voice. "Yeah?"

"Yeah. I'm going to start a charitable trust for abandoned animals and employ myself. I already have a lawyer working on the details. It'll be worthwhile, satisfying work. Next, I'll get a new apartment."

"Sounds like a plan."

"I'm going to be fine."

"Okay."

"No man is that important."

Nash gave her a look that said she was deluding herself. Maybe she was. But it was all she had at the moment.

David shrieked again, as Larry pulled up to the dock. He tied off while the kids pulled the inflatable out of the water and up onto the beach.

"Guess I'd better think about dinner," said Nash, pushing his chair back.

"Never would have guessed you were the domesticated type."

"There are a lot of things you wouldn't guess," he said with a mock, two-fingered salute.

"Auntie Crystal," David called, jogging across the lawn ahead of Larry and Jennifer. "That was cool!"

"Really?" said Crystal. "I couldn't tell you were having fun."

David made it to the top of the stairs. "We were having fun," he confirmed, hopping up and down in place.

"Glad to hear it. Coming up on dinner, so you better get out of that wet bathing suit."

He nodded, scampering for the glass door, remembering to wipe his feet on the mat before heading inside.

Jennifer arrived, her skinny arms wrapped around her bathing suit–clad body. "We're going to need a big dinner," she announced.

"I could eat a horse," said Larry.

"Eeewww," squealed Jennifer, prancing into the house.

Nash appeared in the doorway, his telephone headset in his ear.

He looked at Larry just as Crystal's cell phone rang.

She turned to the table to answer it and thought she saw Nash give Larry a nod.

"Hello?" she greeted.

"Crystal Hayes?"

"Yes?"

"This is Sergeant Wilson of the Charlotte Metropolitan Police. I've been asked to inform you that a Mr. Zane Crandell was taken into custody today. He's here at the Central Station."

A wash of relief fell through Crystal's body, and she dropped herself into a deck chair.

Larry approached, putting a hand on her shoulder.

"Thank you," she said to the man.

"Do you have any questions?"

"No." There was nothing more she wanted to know. Zane was off the streets and that was all that mattered.

"Very well," said the sergeant. "Goodbye, then."

"Goodbye." She gripped the little phone tight. "They got him."

"That's great," said Larry, with a squeeze. "Do you want to tell the kids?"

Crystal pictured their dripping hair and laughing eyes. "Let's do it later."

Larry nodded, and Crystal's phone rang again.

She put it back up to her ear. "Hello?"

"Crystal?" It was her mother.

"You heard? I am so relieved."

"Crystal."

Relief began turning to anger. "Whatever they give him. Whatever he gets—"

"*Crystal.*" Her mother's tone was uncharacteristically sharp.

"What?"

"It's Amber."

Everything inside Crystal went dead still. "What?" she rasped from deep in her chest.

"They had to do emergency surgery."

Time stopped while her mother took a breath.

"She didn't survive it." Stella's voice broke.

"No," Crystal moaned. "No."

How could it happen? How could it have gone so terribly wrong? The relationship should have run its course. Zane should have grown tired and left town.

"It was the bleeding," said her mother, regrouping. "They couldn't stop the bleeding."

David's laughter echoed down the stairs, and Nash immediately retreated inside, closing the door behind him.

Larry's arm went around Crystal's shoulders as the first sob burst from deep in her soul.

CHAPTER FIFTEEN

THE FUNERAL WAS SUNDAY. While his family attended the NASCAR race in Michigan, Larry was in Charlotte, standing in a wind-swept cemetery with a cluster of Amber's friends and family watching Jennifer protectively clutch her little brother who was sitting on a dark, folding chair between his sister and Crystal, tears streaking his cheeks. The little girl was dry-eyed, and had been that way since she heard the terrible news.

Crystal's face was stark white above the collar of her black dress. He knew she'd been busy with the arrangements for the past three days, but it looked like reality had now hit her with a sledgehammer.

The preacher spoke of life, death and redemption, but Larry didn't think Crystal was hearing a word. She stared straight at the polished coffin and its simple bouquet of white roses. Her parents sat next to Jennifer, while the rest of those assembled stood in the early morning sunshine.

Larry knew there was nothing he could do or say that would ease her sorrow. The preacher finished, then the family bravely rose as the coffin was lowered into the ground. They each dropped a rose into the grave, then the other mourners filed by.

Larry said his own goodbye to the woman he'd never had the chance to get to know, then he followed Crystal, catching up to her at the line of black cars waiting at the curb.

While the kids got in, he gently touched her elbow.

She turned.

"If there's anything I can do…"

She nodded and gave him a brave smile, patting his arm. "I'm going to keep it low-key this week."

"Good idea."

"I don't…" Her voice broke. "I don't even know if I should take them home for some of their things, or buy them new clothes. Would familiar things be good, or would the trip traumatize them?"

"Play it by ear," he suggested. "You'll know what to do."

She gave a little nod of uncertainty, looking small and tired and so alone in the world.

His hands curled into fists, and he had to steel himself to keep from drawing her into his arms, lending her his strength, trying everything in his power to take away some of her burden.

But he knew he couldn't do that. Being half in, half out of her life was the worst thing he could do. He could still see the love in her eyes. It matched the adoration he felt in his soul. If there were no complicating factors, he'd whisk her and the kids off right this minute and keep them with him forever.

But life wasn't simple. Hell, there was nothing about life that was remotely simple.

"Thank you, Larry," she whispered, stretching up to kiss him on the cheek.

And then she slipped away. The car door closed, and they pulled away from the curb.

When the car disappeared around the corner, he turned

to walk back to his own car. He put it in gear, drove home and headed straight to his study, forcing himself to take up his research, hoping against hope he could take his mind off Crystal and the kids.

He worked relentlessly every day. But when he was forced to stop to eat, he'd think about Crystal. Several times he picked up the phone, only to slam it back down in self-disgust.

But, as the days wore on, he weakened. He started asking himself what would be so terrible about a call, or about a quick visit? At the very least, he wanted the kids to know he was there for them. And he was. He was prepared to offer anything they needed.

Then, on Friday, he remembered Crystal's overnight bag. It was still in the backseat of his car from the night they broke up. He could return it, say hello to the kids, maybe stay for coffee.

Without giving his better nature a chance to protest, he abandoned his whiteboard and grabbed his car keys.

IT HAD BEEN A QUIET WEEK for Crystal. The first couple of days were the worst, but they were slowly settling into a routine. Amber's will had made it clear that she wanted Crystal to raise her children, and their grandparents supported that wish. The day after the funeral, Crystal's mother had arrived with some of the kids' clothes from their apartment, and wisely arranged to have their beds, quilts and stuffed animals delivered to Crystal's place.

Not for the first time, she appreciated her mother's strength and practicality.

Jennifer and David seemed comforted by the familiar things. David was on-and-off weepy, particularly at night, but Rufus seemed to give him great comfort. Crystal was grateful for the dog. It was the need to walk him that first got her back outside. Yesterday, they'd even done a grocery shopping trip.

Jennifer hadn't cried yet. Crystal had worried about that. But then she read that it was normal. Everyone's grief took a different path.

There was a knock at her kitchen door.

Rufus immediately took up his post.

"Can I get it?" asked Jennifer, looking up from her book.

"Go ahead." Crystal nodded. "But look through the window first."

Jennifer rose and padded across the room. "It's Uncle Larry," she called, joy in her voice.

Crystal's stomach clenched with nerves, while David skidded out from the bedroom. "Uncle Larry?"

Jennifer opened the door, and Crystal came face-to-face with the man who'd been haunting her dreams.

"Hi, guys," he greeted, smiling at each of the kids.

He looked to Crystal and held up her overnight bag. "I thought you might need this."

She'd completely forgotten about leaving the bag in his car. Rising to her feet, she crossed the apartment to take it from his hands. "It was nice of you to bring it by." She felt ridiculously formal and awkward.

"Are you flying today?" asked David.

Larry smiled. "As a matter of fact, I am." A pause. "But not the Cessna. I was thinking about taking the jet to California. There's a NASCAR race there this weekend."

David's jaw dropped open. And really, so did Crystal's.

"You have a jet?" asked David, in a reverent tone.

"It's not mine," Larry warned. "It belongs to my nephew Kent. He said we could use it if we wanted to come and see him race."

David's and Jennifer's eyes were wide and hopeful. They stood perfectly still, attentive to what Larry might say next.

He raised his eyebrows in Crystal's direction.

She gave him a subtle nod. The trip would probably be good for the kids, and she knew Larry would take excellent care of them.

His face lit up with delight. "Would anyone like to come along?"

"Yes!" the children both squealed at the same time. "Can we, Auntie Crystal?"

"Sure, you can. But you have to be good for Uncle Larry."

Three shocked, silent faces turned her way.

"But, you're coming, too, aren't you?" David voiced the question.

"Of course she's coming, too," Larry leapt in. "So is Rufus. My future daughter-in-law has set up a pet area at the track beside her mobile vet unit."

Crystal's heart started to pound. A weekend with Larry? How was that going to work? Could she ignore him and focus on the kids? Did she dare try to rekindle something?

"Let's pack," Jennifer cried, and the kids disappeared, leaving Crystal and Larry staring silently at each other.

"I hope that was okay," said Larry, looking guilty but less than contrite.

"It'll be good for them," Crystal told him honestly.

"And what about you?" His meaning was clear. How would she handle spending time with him?

"They're my priority at the moment." Attempting to adopt her mother's approach to adversity, she moved briskly over to the kitchen table, shutting down her laptop. "I'm going to have to bring some work along. I'm afraid I'll be pretty busy with it."

"I take it all's well with the five million?"

"All is well," she confirmed. "I'm working with a lawyer and an accountant. I decided to manage the trust myself. Pay myself a salary. Maybe buy the kids a house."

"I think that's a great idea," Larry said softly, his eyes conveying admiration. "Bring along all the work you want."

CRYSTAL SHOULD HAVE BEEN working. But there was something peaceful about sitting in the early Saturday morning breeze, watching Jennifer and David play with a group of NASCAR teams kids. They appeared to be friendly and inclusive, and in no time at all, Jennifer and David were caught up in the games.

Crystal had found a bench, shaded by one of the haulers. Clouds scuttled across the blue sky, the temperature was cool, and the garage area was a pleasant hum in the distance. She took the first relaxed breath she'd allowed herself all week.

Then a figure appeared in her peripheral vision.

Steve Grosso.

She saw that he'd spotted her, hesitated, then made up his mind and marched toward her.

Her heart sank. She really wasn't up for an argument.

His feet came to a halt next to the bench. "Hello, Crystal."

She pretended to notice him for the first time. "Steve."

He gestured to the bench. "Do you mind?"

Yes. "Of course not."

He took a seat, and they were silent for a few minutes.

"I was sorry to hear about your sister."

She nodded, keeping her vision straight ahead.

"I remember how painful it was to lose my mother." He

took a breath, watching the children play. "I promise, it gets better. Slowly. But day by day, week by week. The raw pain subsides, and you eventually find a new normal."

"That's what I need," she told him in a strained voice. "A new normal." For her and for the kids.

Silence took over again.

Then Steve cleared his throat. "I realize you weren't after my father's money."

The words surprised Crystal, and she turned to look at him. There was pain and regret in his expression. "Heidi, my fiancée, told me about your animal trust. She said you told her all about it when you dropped your dog off." He paused again. "I owe you a very big apology."

"Thank you," she managed.

"I don't know what I can—"

"It's over," Crystal put in. "Your dad's made up his mind."

"But—"

"It wasn't you, or your opinion. He wants me to find a man my own age, to have children." She gave a cold laugh at the absurdity of Larry's fantasy.

"I accused him of having a midlife crisis."

"Maybe he was," Crystal allowed. Larry had claimed he was breaking up for her own good. But who could guess the real reason? Maybe he'd fulfilled whatever twenty-something-year-itch had hit him, and he was done with her. She'd never know for sure.

"That's absurd," said Steve.

"How do you know?"

"Because I know my father. I'm going to—"

"Don't," she told him sharply. "Please. Walk away from it." Her gaze went back to the kids. "I have enough to deal with at the moment."

"Right," he agreed, rising to his feet. "Once again, I'm very sorry. I made a very big mistake."

"Thank you."

"WELL, THAT WAS PROBABLY the stupidest thing you've ever done," said Milo. The family's racing patriarch was holding court outside Dean's motor home while race cars qualified on the track in front of them.

Larry didn't bother disagreeing with his grandfather's assessment of his actions with Crystal.

"Juliana's fifteen years younger than me," Milo continued. "That ever cause us any problems?"

Larry looked to his brother Dean, who had also been raised by Milo and Juliana. "Not that I could see," Larry allowed, and Dean nodded.

Just then, Juliana came out of the motor home.

"My age a problem for you?" Milo demanded.

"Only that you won't grow up," Juliana put in smoothly. "Am I to understand we're talking about the Larry and Crystal situation?"

Larry wasn't wild about being described as a "situation," but he wouldn't be rude to the woman who'd been both mother and grandmother to him. "What about children of her own?" he had to ask, knowing Juliana had never had her own children.

"You'll have to ask her that question," Juliana answered softly. "When we finally met her this morning, she seemed like a lovely girl. Smart enough, maybe, to know that life doesn't come in a neat little package. A person is lucky to find love at all, never mind find love in the perfect circumstance.

"I never gave birth, but that doesn't mean I didn't have children. It seems to me the young lady we're talking about *has* children. Maybe she wants more, maybe she doesn't. But she could probably use a hand with the two she's got."

Understanding suddenly slammed into Larry.

Crystal needed him here and now. She was living her real life, not some fantasy he'd conjured up for her. He loved her. He had to support her, make her happy and help her with whatever burdens life threw her way.

What he should do and what he wanted to do, were exactly the same thing. For a genius, he sure was slow on the uptake sometimes.

"Dad," came Steve's breathless voice, as he raced to the circle of lawn chairs. "I was wrong."

"About what?" asked Kent.

"About Crystal," said Steve.

"No kidding," said Larry.

"You need to make up with her. You need to…marry her and help her with those kids. If you don't march over there right now and offer to share her life, you're not the father I thought you were."

"You want me to propose to her?"

"Yes!" came a chorus from those assembled.

"In the infield?" Larry was up for the proposal part, but he didn't think it needed to happen in the next five minutes. Or maybe it did. Suddenly, he couldn't wait.

"She's over by the play area," Steve offered, his breathing back to normal.

Larry hesitated.

But then Juliana came forward, pressing something into the palm of his hand.

He looked down to see her gold, solitaire engagement ring.

"No," he protested, vehemently shaking his head.

But she closed his hand around the ring. "What, are they going to bury me with it?"

"Nobody's burying you anytime soon," said Larry.

Juliana just smiled, with perfect contentment. "I'll keep the wedding band. But there's something about this young woman that reminds me of me." She winked at Larry, while Milo pulled her back into his lap.

"Do as my young wife tells you," groused Milo.

Larry tightened his hand around the ring, butterflies forming in his stomach. What if she wasn't ready to forgive him? What if she said no? Worse, what if she'd decided he was right and she should hold out for somebody younger?

He hesitated, but Steve pointed him in the direction of the play area and gave him a gentle shove.

STILL WATCHING THE KIDS PLAY, Crystal caught another figure in her peripheral vision.

Larry, this time.

She steeled her emotions for his arrival, something she'd practiced a lot, but pretty much sucked at.

Her heart rate increased as he sat down on the bench beside her.

"How're they doing?" he asked, with a nod toward the children.

As always, his deep voice sent a shiver down her spine.

"Better," she told him.

He stretched his arm along the length of the back, brushing against her hair, nearly making her jump out of her skin.

"I never meant to make things hard for you," he said.

She nodded. "I know. It was nice of you to invite the kids. I think it's been good for them."

"Crystal?"

"Yes?"

"Look at me."

She gathered her defenses and turned her head.

His eyes were clear and honest in the sunlight. "That's not what I meant."

She waited.

"Tell me something," he said.

"What?"

"If it was up to you, where would our relationship go?"

Her stomach hollowed out. What was his game?

"Seriously," he prompted.

"Don't do this," she hissed.

His eyes darkened further, and he inched a little closer. "I need to know," he intoned.

"I haven't changed my mind," she said.

"And that means?"

"That means—" she glared at him defiantly "—if it was up to me, if nobody else got a vote, you, me, Jennifer and David would live happily ever after."

"I was kind of hoping you'd say that."

"Why?" she spat out, seriously considering getting up to leave.

"Because, I love you."

She waved a dismissive hand. "Fat lot of good that's ever done me."

"And," Larry drew a deep breath, apparently choosing to ignore her mood. "I want you to marry me."

She opened her mouth to retaliate, but then the words registered, and her jaw dropped.

He opened his hand, and she saw a small ring nestled in his palm.

Her eyes flew to his, her mouth forming into an O.

"Marry me, Crystal. I love you, and I don't care what anyone thinks or says. If you'll take me without babies, I'm yours for the rest of my life."

"Auntie Crystal," David called in a happy voice, and she could see the two children running toward her.

"What do you say?" asked Larry.

Her heart sang, and tears of joy formed in her eyes. "I say yes. I say you're stuck with me. And I say we've already got two beautiful children."

"Auntie Crystal?" David repeated, and she turned to look at him.

He took in her face. "What's wrong?"

"Nothing's wrong," said Larry. "I just asked Auntie Crystal to marry me." He paused. "And she said yes."

"You're getting married?" asked Jennifer, coming to a halt, her expression wary.

Larry nodded, but Crystal paused, watching the girl closely.

"So," said David, his lips pursing as he moved toward Larry. His little chest expanded with a slow breath. "It'll be like you're my dad, but with a plane?"

"Yes," said Larry soberly. "It'll be exactly like that."

David whooped and threw himself into Larry's arms.

Larry's eyes closed, and he held David's little body tight against his chest, his arms wrapped protectively around him.

Jennifer had stayed silent, and Crystal glanced her way again.

The young girl's shoulders were shaking.

"Sweetheart," Crystal asked, leaning toward her, frightened.

Jennifer stared at David in Larry's arms. Relief flooded her expression, and she choked on a sob.

Suddenly Crystal got it.

Jennifer had been holding it together for her little brother. She'd been protecting him for so long, she didn't know how to stop. She couldn't grieve herself, because she didn't know if David was going to need her.

Crystal pulled the shaking girl into her arms, holding her tight while Jennifer buried her face in Crystal's neck.

"Larry's going to be there for David," she whispered. "And I'm going to be there. And Grandma and Grandpa, and Larry's entire family. We're all going to make sure David's okay."

Jennifer nodded against her shoulder, the tears and sobs flowing freely.

For long minutes, Crystal simply held her.

Larry's and David's voices were low murmurs next to them on the bench.

Finally, the girl's grief seemed to ebb.

"Is Mommy in Heaven?" Jennifer's small, watery voice asked against Crystal's damp shoulder.

"Mommy," Crystal managed, "is most certainly in Heaven."

"And my dad is going to stay in jail?"

"Yes."

Jennifer reached a small, shaking hand inside the pocket of her shorts and retrieved the little black cell phone. "Then I don't need this anymore?"

Crystal's hand closed around the phone, her chest squeezing with pain. "No, honey. You don't need it anymore."

Crystal's gaze caught Larry's as a deep, shuddering breath of relief whooshed out of Jennifer's lungs.

The little girl still had some crying to do. And they

would grieve together for a long while to come. But there was a bright new future waiting for all four of them.

Crystal reached for Larry's hand, and it joined solidly with her own.

* * * * *

*For more thrill-a-mile romances set against
the exciting backdrop of the NASCAR world, don't miss:
TEAMING UP by Abby Gaines.
Available in August.
For a sneak peek, just turn the page!*

"WHY DID YOU ASK ME OUT?" WADE SAID. "You didn't really have the hots for me, did you?"

"You're very attractive," Kim said fairly, then paused. "It was a spur-of-the-moment thing."

"You don't do spur of the moment."

How had he figured that out?

"The old me didn't do spur of the moment," she said. "The new me—"

"Why do you need a new you?" he interrupted. "What was wrong with the old one?"

"The old one's life was too tame," she said. "I wanted to do something…adventurous. Then I saw you." She spread her hands as if the rest was obvious.

"Asking a guy to have coffee is your idea of adventurous?" He shook his head, disbelieving. "Did you think about skydiving?"

"It's all relative."

He was looking at her as if she had the courage of a bowl of jelly. In self-defense, suddenly anxious that he shouldn't think her pathetic, Kim reached into her purse and pulled out the folded list that she now carried everywhere, like a talisman against her boring life.

She waved it at him. "If I'd been starting from scratch

I'm sure I'd have planned something more challenging.
But I came across a list I wrote back in college and that
triggered my decision."

Wade rubbed his chin. "What kind of list?"

She gnawed on her lower lip. "You have to know where
I was coming from when I wrote it. I fast-tracked through
high school and college, so I never got to do a lot of the
things other girls did."

"You mean—" he leaned forward, interested now
"—things like, make out at the movies?"

Kim gaped, shielding the list with her hand as if it had
suddenly turned transparent. "How did you know?"

He laughed, and the deep, attractive sound turned heads
at nearby tables. "*Everyone* made out at the movies."

"I didn't," she said crossly. "And could you keep your
voice down? The whole restaurant doesn't need to know
I'm a loser."

His look was speculative, but he said more quietly,
"What else didn't you do?"

She gripped the list tighter. "I'm not telling."

It soon became obvious who was the big, strong
NASCAR car chief around here and who was the puny scientist. In one swift movement he snatched the list from her.

"Give that back." She tried to grab it, but her arms were
shorter than his.

Wade began reading. Almost immediately, his lips
twitched, and he darted a quick glance at Kim. Somewhere lower than her face. *The push-up bra.* Hastily, she
folded her arms across her chest, and his smile widened.

"You've seen the list," she said. "Now I'd like it back."

Wade read down the list with a frown that deepened.
And deepened. Kim braced herself.

She knew when he got there. His head shot up: accusation burned in his dark eyes. "You asked me to dinner because you want to date a jock?"

REQUEST YOUR FREE BOOKS!

2 FREE NOVELS PLUS 2 FREE GIFTS!

Silhouette®

SPECIAL EDITION®

Life, Love and Family!

YES! Please send me 2 FREE Silhouette Special Edition® novels and my 2 FREE gifts (gifts are worth about $10). After receiving them, if I don't wish to receive any more books, I can return the shipping statement marked "cancel." If I don't cancel, I will receive 6 brand-new novels every month and be billed just $4.24 per book in the U.S. or $4.99 per book in Canada, plus 25¢ shipping and handling per book and applicable taxes, if any*. That's a savings of at least 15% off the cover price! I understand that accepting the 2 free books and gifts places me under no obligation to buy anything. I can always return a shipment and cancel at any time. Even if I never buy another book from Silhouette, the two free books and gifts are mine to keep forever.

235 SDN EEYU   335 SDN EEY6

Name	(PLEASE PRINT)	

Address		Apt. #

City	State/Prov.	Zip/Postal Code

Signature (if under 18, a parent or guardian must sign)

Mail to the Silhouette Reader Service:
IN U.S.A.: P.O. Box 1867, Buffalo, NY 14240-1867
IN CANADA: P.O. Box 609, Fort Erie, Ontario L2A 5X3

Not valid to current subscribers of Silhouette Special Edition books.

**Want to try two free books from another line?
Call 1-800-873-8635 or visit www.morefreebooks.com.**

* Terms and prices subject to change without notice. N.Y. residents add applicable sales tax. Canadian residents will be charged applicable provincial taxes and GST. Offer not valid in Quebec. This offer is limited to one order per household. All orders subject to approval. Credit or debit balances in a customer's account(s) may be offset by any other outstanding balance owed by or to the customer. Please allow 4 to 6 weeks for delivery. Offer available while quantities last.

Your Privacy: Silhouette is committed to protecting your privacy. Our Privacy Policy is available online at www.eHarlequin.com or upon request from the Reader Service. From time to time we make our lists of customers available to reputable third parties who may have a product or service of interest to you. If you would prefer we not share your name and address, please check here. ☐

SSE08R

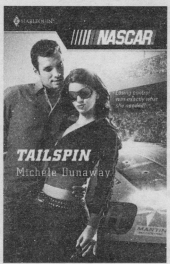